CLAIMING HIS WITCH

FERAL BREED MOTORCYCLE CLUB
BOOK THREE

ELLIS LEIGH

Kinship Press

To my husband, who continually reminds me to stop working and disconnect for awhile before I miss everything. And who makes me popcorn when I ask for it.

ONE

I FLEW DOWN THE two-lane highway, the cold November wind burning my face. Dropping down into every curve and pushing the speedometer higher on the straightaways, I raced time with two wheels rolling along asphalt. Letting my thoughts roam, my mind wander, and my heart enjoy the ride.

This was my favorite part of being with the Feral Breed Motorcycle Club. The freedom that came from knowing death was much farther away than it was before I'd been turned. Not that there was no chance of going lights-out. Even as a wolf shifter, I'd almost died after making a stupid mistake on a mission with my Breed brothers. And yet, as I pushed my bobber past the hundred-mile-an-hour mark and leaned hard into a sharp turn in the road, I felt bulletproof. Confident. Nothing could stop me. Nothing could rein me in. Nothing could knock me off-balance. Not when I was on two wheels or four paws.

It was only the human side of me that still seemed to lose his balance as I roared my way through this life.

Physical balance had not been kind to me as a child. I'd fallen and skinned my knees countless times, taken a tumble down a flight of stairs, even busted an ankle tripping over a stick hidden in the tall grass of the fields around the trailer where I grew up. Balance had definitely bitch-slapped me a time or two. It still slithered out of my grasp at times, though no longer in the physical sense of the word. More balance between my past and my present; my human life and my shifter life; what the two sides of me wanted to be at any given time.

As a wolf shifter in the Feral Breed, I knew my role. I was a prospect; biding my time and doing everything I could to prove my worth to the patched members. My goal was in sight— the addition of a Feral Breed MC rocker and a growling wolf insignia to the black leather I always wore. We were guardians of the secret, protectors of our fellow wolf shifters, and I wanted that patch more than anything I'd ever wanted in my life. I was focused, I was on target, and I knew exactly what I needed to do.

As a human man, I had a tendency to lose myself in memories and regrets. I'd almost died for a mistake my human side made, ignoring both the orders I'd been given and my wolf instincts. If not for the damage a deranged shifter had inflicted on me, I probably would have lost my spot in the Feral Breed. I'd let my leader down, I'd let his mate down, I'd let my Brothers down, and I'd disrespected my wolf spirit. I'd nearly lost everything, but I was on a mission to right my wrongs. I would make it up to my team. I would earn that patch.

Even if trying brought death back to my doorstep.

I slowed to a more reasonable speed as I rolled in to the town where I grew up. The place looked the same—single stoplight, empty buildings on the main business strip, pallor of poverty hanging in the air like the stink of rotting garbage on a hot day. This place made my skin itch and my wolf spirit prick his proverbial ears. Not that there was anything special about it. This place was a town like many others, like any based in a region where factory closings had caused businesses—and then families of the unemployed—to wither and die.

My hometown sat seven miles from the shore of Lake Michigan. On the coast, people found a strip of land filled with tourists and transplants who could afford a life on the beach. But drive inland, and instead of big houses and trendy restaurants, one found a bunch of little towns just like this. Shabby, decaying, and practically hidden from the eyes of the people driving past on the expressways.

Growling to myself, I tightened my grip on the throttle and clenched my jaw. I couldn't get lost in my memories of this place. I needed to stay focused on my job, not wonder about the things I'd left behind. This trip was to be one hundred percent about work, even if I'd be working right where my old life had ended and my new one began.

Once past the only operating gas station in town, I turned off the main drag and headed down a side street to the shop owned by Beast, brother of the Gatekeeper, and the man who made me what I was. Pulling into the Yard Shark Customs driveway was like stepping into a time warp, one that did its best to knock me right back into those memories trying to pull me off course. The asphalt gleamed dark and unblemished from the edge of the road all the way up to the bay doors. The hulking corpses of various classic cars waiting for whatever magic they needed to make them roadworthy lined the fences, each perfectly placed with a near-obsessive attention to spacing. Not much had changed since the first time I'd rolled onto the lot nearly sixteen years ago, an eager kid looking for something to do to make a little money and keep busy during the summer break from school. I'd had no clue what turning onto that lot would eventually lead to. And I'd had no foresight that returning would make me feel like I'd been kicked in the junk.

I parked my bike in front of one of the bay doors and paused a moment to take it all in. Brown, barn-wood exterior, black roll-up doors, and boisterous fall-colored flowers in containers lining the front walkway, interspersed with pumpkins of various sizes. Clean and welcoming, the shop looked like any average, middle-America small business. Which made it way too nice for the town around it.

It was also nearly impenetrable.

There was no way to sneak onto Yard Shark land without alerting the security system. The owner had made sure of that after the breach that brought me to my new life. If there was one way I was exactly like my maker, it was in that—I might make a mistake, but I'd learn from my error. It wouldn't happen twice. His biggest mistake had been not paying enough attention the night a nomad came to town; mine had been not paying enough attention to my inner wolf. I'd paid for his mistake with my human life; I was still paying for my own.

I stood and swung my leg over the seat as the man who'd been my boss, my friend, my teacher, and, in the end, my wolf giver, appeared in the open bay door to my left. "What's up, brother?"

"Not a whole helluva lot, Pup. You do know it's supposed to snow, right?" Beast nodded toward my bike. I grinned. I knew it was a gamble riding it up, but I couldn't resist one more trip before the snow fell and we were stuck waiting for the world to thaw.

"You know me, man. I'm all about taking risks."

Beast snorted. "Sure thing, kid. Keep telling yourself that. What're you doing up this way? I didn't expect to see you until the big feast at the end of the month."

He ambled outside as he wiped his greasy hands on a dirty, red rag. The black skullcap he wore sported the Feral Breed insignia sans rockers. The same insignia was tattooed on his forearm amidst a swirling pattern of lines and images. People saw the Beast—with his full-sleeves and the wicked scar curving up the side of his face—and they assumed he was dangerous. And he was, as all wolf shifters were. But he was also kind and compassionate; a quiet man with a deep sense of what was right and wrong. I was living proof of that.

"I had some work to do out this way, so Rebel sent me to see you. Said I needed to make sure the bagger was put through its paces before he picked it up this weekend. He should be rolling in to the lake camp later tonight." I strolled toward the garage, fighting back the memories with each step.

"Custom rides take time. You and Rebel know that." Beast gave me a backslapping hug before directing us inside.

I shrugged. "I think he's anxious to get back to work. He doesn't have a bike he deems"—I made air quotes—"good enough for his Cherry."

Beast huffed. "The boy's got about fifteen skids that would be right comfortable for someone on a bitch seat. Now he wants a bagger with a behemoth motor, to what? Chase down man-eaters with his human mate on the back?"

"Don't ask me, man. I just do what I'm told."

"You Anbizens don't make a lot of sense sometimes." Beast looked my way, his face growing serious. "So the mating went well, I assume? She take to him okay?"

"Seems so. We haven't seen either one of them in months. Shadow and I rode through Milwaukee to check on them before the weather turned cold, but we couldn't get close to the door." I smirked and raised an eyebrow. "Cherry started screaming whenever we stepped foot on her property."

"What was she yelling for?"

My smirk morphed into a full-on grin. "Well, at that particular moment, she was yelling for more, for him to go faster, and occasionally hollering out the Lord's name."

Beast bellowed a laugh, the sound echoing through the

concrete-floored structure. "You tried walking up to the den of a newly mated wolf while he was fucking his woman? You're lucky you didn't get a chunk taken out of your ass."

"It's not like I knew what they were up to. When we rolled up, they were quiet. But that quiet didn't last long."

"Well, damn. Good for Rebel. I'm real happy for him." Beast shook his head as we walked between pits. "Man, I'm going to razz that kid hard when he gets his ass up here. All mated and riding a bagger, for fuck's sake. I thought only that chump Magnus would ever ride one of these giants for the Detroit den."

We came to the back alcove where a turquoise and white motorcycle rested on the lift. Sleek and long, the bike was showstoppingly gorgeous. From the huge front wheel to the low handlebars, the white leather seat to the chrome accents, Rebel's new toy would definitely be turning heads.

I whistled low. "She sure is a looker."

Beast nodded before pulling his skullcap off and dropping it on the workbench. "She is, and she's going to ride like a motherfucking La-Z-Boy once she gets rolling. But just like any woman, she's been giving me shit all damn day. I can't get the wiring right to save my sorry ass."

"She won't start?"

"Oh no, she'll start. I just can't get her to finish." He chuckled at his own innuendo before pointing toward the engine. "She putters out every time I put her in gear."

I ran my fingers over the curve of the large front headlight. "Think it's the wiring?"

"This ain't my first rodeo, boy."

Memories of the night the purely human me died flooded my mind. The blood and pain from the attack that had forced Beast to turn me, even though he didn't think I was ready. The way the world seemed to tear itself apart and put itself back together as I writhed on the cot in the far back corner of the garage. The confusion that had filled my consciousness as I'd come to, no longer just human inside my own mind. And Beast, calm as ever, looking me over and snorting.

"Don't even think of attacking me, boy. This ain't my first rodeo."

I grunted and reached for the work light hanging from the ceiling. "Pretty sure I've heard that line before."

His eyes met mine, a look of regret arguing with the slight smile tugging up the unscarred side of his face. "Pretty sure you'll hear it again." Beast pointed to the bike. "I think if we can get the wiring right, this girl'll be ready to ride."

"Then let's get to work."

We worked for hours, disassembling, investigating, and following every assembly step backward to find the problem. I'd learned how to build a work of art from nothing more than sheet metal and discarded parts long ago—over summers and school breaks when I'd spent every moment in the shop, working metal, and breathing in the fumes of mineral spirits and gasoline. Beast had taught me the basics of the combustion engine, how to tell what was wrong with one, and how to fix it to run the way it was meant to. He'd taught me to take a sheet of metal and turn it into a custom gas tank, how to take steel tubing and bend it into a frame that would eventually become a custom bike.

He'd also taught me about being responsible and earning your keep. He taught me what it meant to be a man, filling a void left by the parents who'd kicked me out when I was only fifteen. Beast had come to my rescue, and for seven years, he'd taught me the ways of engines and metal and life. He'd rescued me from a life of poverty and ignorance, giving me a skill in the hope that I'd have a successful future. And then he'd come to my rescue again, and my education had turned a little more lupine in nature.

"Kickstand wires." My blurted words were met with a look of confusion. "When we got called over to Grand Haven that time, the guy's chopper had a similar issue. It was a bad connection in the kickstand wires."

Beast grinned as he crouched beside the bike. "Damn, boy. I'd forgotten all about that."

"Yeah, well"—I shrugged and smiled—"you've been around a lot longer than me."

"That I have, my friend. That I have."

Half an hour later, Beast was riding the bagger around the building, making sure the thing handled as expected. It looked good going down the road, like an aggressive motorcycle riff on a fifties-style race car. Reb's bike was the opposite of my bobber—all decked out and chromed up with room for luggage. My baby was as stripped as you could get. No turn signals, no fancy exhaust, or custom headlight. The only nonessential feature on my bobber was the extra seat on the back, and even that had led to a fight between Beast and me when we were building her. He called it necessary; I called it an extravagance. He won that one, but the rest of the bike was all me. My style—simple, functional, and only what was necessary.

I'd just finished putting away the welding supplies for the night when Beast rode back into the shop. I winced at the sound bouncing around the room, the noise level making me want to flee. Something I'd never experienced. Usually, the louder the exhaust, the more I liked the bike. This time, I physically recoiled from the roar.

After Beast quieted the engine and I took a moment to calm the anxiousness running through me, I brought the conversation to Feral Breed business. I needed to force my mind off the way my nerves were jangling in my brain.

"You been hanging out at the K-zoo den?"

Beast shrugged. "Not much, really. I've had a lot of custom orders keeping me busy. Why? What's up?"

"Guess there's a bit of trouble with one of the members. Seems some of the money from Draught sales turned up missing, and now their treasurer's in the wind."

The Draught, Rebel's concoction that worked as a suppressant for our wolf instincts, was how the Feral Breed made a vast majority of our money. We brewed it, packaged it, and sold it. Nonaddictive, the drug was a boon to all the shifters trying to fit in to the human world. It also kept us Anbizen, or turned shifters, from falling completely to our wolf instincts and becoming man-eaters. Something relatively common in our world.

"Who's their treasurer these days?"

"Man named Spook. You know him?"

"Yeah, yeah, I do. But he's not your guy." Beast grabbed the handful of tools littering our work area and walked across the room to the tool chest. "Spook's about as honest as they come. He's not one to steal, and he sure as hell isn't one to run."

I hummed in response, unsure of what to say. Beast was a great judge of character, but Spook failed to turn in a huge chunk of the monthly earn and disappeared. No calls, no notes, no sign of foul play at his home according to the enforcer of their group. Seemed like a simple grab-and-dash job to me, but I'd keep Beast's opinion in mind. I definitely needed to do a little digging once I headed down to K-zoo in the morning.

"You meet Gates' mate yet?" I asked, ready for a subject change.

"Yeah." Beast closed the top of the tool chest and turned toward me, smiling. "They came out here on their way to Detroit. She's a pretty little thing."

"That she is." I walked to the sink in the back corner and scrubbed the grease off my hands. The sudden anxiety was back, giving me the sense of a storm building nearby. Something new and possibly dangerous. It wasn't a feeling I was used to dealing with, this edginess about nothing tangible. I shook it off again, trying to hide my nervousness from Beast. "She's strong, though. Tough. I think she'll be a good match for him."

Beast joined me at the sink, washing his hands in the second basin. "Two men down in a matter of months. That's got to be rough on the dens."

I shrugged and reached for a shop towel with shaky hands. "We're dealing, though it's hard to keep things in check between the two dens. That's why this Kalamazoo thing is such a bite to the ass—it's pretty much our own fault for not watching the satellite denhouse closer."

"You can't be everywhere at once, kid." His eyes dropped to where I was gripping the towel. "How's it going at the Detroit den?"

"Been quiet for a while. Magnus is spending the winter at the Fields. His knee healed wrong and the docs keep having to rebreak it. Sucks for him, but the rest of the guys are happier without him around. Especially since we don't have to hang at the shithole building on the southwest side anymore."

Beast watched as I dried my hands, definitely noticing the tremors but not commenting. The man had the patience of Job.

"Half Trac still on suspension?" Beast's voice came out with a touch of a growl to it, his anger at the backstabbing shifter apparent.

"From what I hear, Blaze has him in the lower level of the Fields and won't let him out. Some kind of isolation punishment."

Beast huffed and hung the towel on the front of the sink. "Good riddance. You don't risk the life of another wolf's mate."

Once everything was back where it belonged, we walked through the shop, turning off lights as we headed for the front.

Beast grabbed a set of keys off a hook by the door before shaking his head.

"My brother waited a long time to find that little girl. If anything had happened to her because Mister Big Shot thought he could come up with a better plan than the rest of the team, he'd be up for a full NALB investigation. He's lucky Gates and the rest of you didn't kill him where he stood."

Beast was right—Half Trac, our National President's second-in-command, had put Gates' mate in some serious danger. Had all of us not been there to help, Gates may very well have lost her before they could finalize their mating. Half Trac was facing serious Feral Breed punishment, as well as possible court hearings with the overseers of the wolf shifters, the National Association of the Lycan Brotherhood.

"There wasn't much any of us could do until Kaija's Omega-voodoo helped overpower the guy. Fucker Alpha-ordered us."

We walked out into the crisp late-afternoon air, waiting as the door came down so Beast could set the alarms.

"I wish I would have been there. No one's been able to Alpha-order me since I was a kid." He smirked as he pulled his Feral Breed cap over his dark hair. "Guess that's a benefit of growing up the little brother of the Gatekeeper."

"You need to teach me that skill." I slipped on my gloves and shivered as snow began to fall. Being part wolf, I loved running through the snow-covered woods in the middle of winter, but I had a fur coat on then. Standing outside on a snowy evening meant only one thing in human form—it was damned cold.

"Hey." Beast's heavy hand landed on my shoulder. "Half Trac was the one who fucked up, not you. I know you feel as if you need to pay some debt by protecting the ladies mated to your Breed brothers, but that's not the case. We all know what happened in Milwaukee wasn't your fault."

Milwaukee…where my bad decision had nearly cost Rebel's mate her life, and I'd been left for dead in a freezer. Feeling a sudden need to shift into my wolf form, I clenched my jaw and stepped away from him.

"Maybe not, but it was still a stupid mistake." I turned and walked toward my bike. "Forget this heavy stuff, man. Let's head over to the lake and see if Reb's made it up yet. I need a drink and a night around the fire pit. Something's making my wolf twitchy."

Beast stepped in front of me; the way he could move without making a sound was something I'd never gotten used to. He peered at me for a few long seconds, his face stoic in the bright light of the moon hanging nearly full in the sky.

My nerves quieted as they always did when he stood this close. Staring at his jaw to keep from making eye contact, a sign of aggression in wolves and shifters, I recognized how much he'd look like his brother if it weren't for the scar and the ink. Where Gates was clean-cut, looking more like a fashion model than a biker, Beast was more rough and damaged—the stereotypical biker badass. But they both had the same shape to their face, the same bright blue eyes. When you looked past the superficial differences, they looked so much alike, they could have been twins.

The brothers were also two of the most loyal people I'd ever met, whether human or shifter. I'd fight for either one of them; die for them if I had to. But because of our history together, Beast would always be the one who would come first in my mind.

Finally, after a proper inspection, Beast made a chuffing sound of approval. He turned and ambled toward his truck, quiet and accepting that I was just off, not losing any of the control he'd taught me. I followed him across the lot, shoving the burning, anxious feeling in my gut down as I went.

"I can come back for Reb's bike tomorrow. Let's throw yours in the back of the truck." Beast dropped the tailgate on his truck. "I don't feel like watching you freeze your balls off because you decided one more trip on your skid would be a good idea."

"Thanks for thinking about my balls, old man."

TWO

Azurine

I WAS LOST. NOT literally, but mentally. Physically, I knew exactly where I was—standing on the shore of Lake Michigan, watching the cold waves roll in and kiss the sandy beach. We'd been enjoying a warm autumn in the region, but winter was coming. Already, the days were short and the dark of night descended long before dinner. We'd been waking up to frost on the ground lately, a reminder that the time of the harvest was long gone. It was the season of rest, a time when the earth slept and death came to the soil and many of the plants we relied on.

I should have been helping my coven dig up those plants and bring them inside the warmth and safety of the greenhouse for repotting, but something had captured my attention and wouldn't let go. Something warming in the chilly November air, bright and hot like a fire on a winter night. Something that felt as strong as the magick that flowed through me.

South south south we must go south we must go now

The pull that had drawn me toward the water since my very first memory—the evidence of the water magick that lived within me—had made itself present earlier in the day. It called to me, asked me to revitalize my connection to the power of the waves. But then it had grown, bastardizing itself into something else. Something stronger. Usually, the sensation was soft and wavelike, ebbing and flowing within me until I satisfied the need by spending time at the shore or in the lake. This time it had been brutal—nearly violent in the way it insisted I get up, get moving, get to wherever it wanted me to be. And that place was not here, not at my home, not standing at the edge of the lake I was raised on. Not on the shore or in the waves.

For centuries, the coven I belonged to had owned a small lighthouse on the shore of the inland sea known as Lake Michigan. The light guarded a strait leading to the much smaller, Lake Parity. I was happily surrounded by water on three sides on this piece of land, but that wasn't enough for the need clawing at my gut. It wanted me to go south, the only direction I could travel without crossing a waterway. The need wanted me to hurry, to run, to go immediately.

And there was no way I could have been prepared for the desperation it caused within me.

"I think we've finally harvested the last of the carrots," Siobhan called, pulling me from my musings and forcing me to focus on what was going on around me instead of staring southward.

Sarah, Siobhan's aunt and the elderly witch who'd raised my sisters and me, dug her fingers deep in the soil. Closing her eyes, she whispered a chant that made the hair on my arms stand on end. Her earth magick was strong, stronger than the rest of the coven put together. It was why we saw her as a leader and why my mother had left us with her when she died.

The soil darkened as Sarah chanted, my sister Amber kneeling by her side. All magick needed balance. A powerful earth witch could lose herself in the seductive pull of the life within the soil if not for the presence of an air witch to keep her grounded. Amber and Sarah worked well together, and each was more powerful in their magick because of the other. Even though Sarah was fifty years older than Amber, theirs was similar to the relationship between my sister Scarlett and me. Her fire magick balanced my water magick in a way that made us each stronger when we worked as a team.

"Merry meet again." Sarah opened her eyes as she whispered the release to the powers of the earth, pulling her hands out of the soil. She looked up at the darkening sky with a frown. "I think it's time to end this day, ladies. If everyone will grab a couple of the uprooted plants, we can have the yard cleaned up quickly. Repotting can wait until the morning."

The other members of our coven, three families totaling eighteen women, each grabbed a few straggly plants or root balls and headed for the glass structure at the back of the lighthouse. Scarlett, the youngest of us Weaver triplets, waited by my side as Sarah and Amber walked our way. Sarah stopped directly in front of me, reaching out to brush one dirty finger down the side of my face. Her eyes were sharp, almost invasive in the way they evaluated me. I blinked and took a deep breath. How she knew I was struggling with something was a mystery, but it spoke to her strength, her power, and her insight into the women of her coven.

"What's going on with you? Your aura is a mess, child." She squinted, the wrinkles around her eyes forming a pattern of lines and swirls that only added to her beauty. Her intense scrutiny calmed me in a way nothing else could. Sarah had led this coven for decades before stepping aside when cancer began its slow overtaking of her body. Even as ill as she was, she radiated knowledge and strength. She may not have been the high priestess any longer, but she would know what to do. She would know what power was making me feel such a pull and how to handle it.

I opened my mouth to speak, but another person suddenly

invaded our space.

"The hunter is near; we should leave this town."

"Nonsense." Sarah turned. "I refuse to abandon my home because you saw a dog in the woods."

Clara Gardner, one of the oldest witches in our coven and one of the three current coven elders, straightened her shoulders and peered back at Sarah. "It was not a dog. It was a hunter in his wolf form. I watched that man turn into that beast and stalk around the lighthouse. The hounds are here to hunt us; you would be wise to listen to my warning."

Sarah sighed and looked to Amber. Air magick enhanced the natural intuition of a witch, making my sister, born with the element of air as the base of her magick, quite the crutch when anything happened around the coven. And the possibility of witch hunters in the area was no different.

"I can't tell you if a hunter is in the area, though there's definitely a dark energy near." Amber glanced at Clara. "I'm sorry. I wish I could say I felt something more, but I can't get a clear picture."

"You don't see anything at all?" Sarah asked.

Amber thought for a moment. "Not really. It's very… fuzzy—I guess that would be the way to describe it. It's as if I run into a veil of some sort."

Sarah frowned, exaggerating the wrinkles around her mouth. "I think tonight would be a good time for meditation, Amber. I could use a little extra rest myself. Maybe all this preparation for winter has us distracted."

Amber didn't look convinced as she stared at the lighthouse. "Could be. It's just so"—she brought her hand up, fingers tracing wavy shapes in the air—"smoky."

"I know how frustrating it can be when you feel blocked." Sarah gave Amber's hand a squeeze before turning back to Clara. The older witch did not look happy.

"Don't you dare dismiss my concerns, Sarah Bishop."

"I'm not; I'm simply asking for a little time to work out what's happening. Let us have the night—Amber will meditate to clear her mind and perhaps get a better idea of this dark energy she feels. None of us wants to deal with a witch hunter, but I refuse to leave my home without some kind of proof we're in danger. Something other than a wolf in the woods."

Clara glared for a few seconds before sighing and nodding her head. "Fine, but be quick about it. A witch hunter waits for no one."

Sarah nodded before turning her gray eyes on me. "And what's happening with you? Your energy's all over the place."

I sighed, the draw to the mystery *something* making me crazy, like an itch I couldn't reach. "I feel a pull, a strong one. It wants me to go south."

"Still?" Sarah looked at me with concern.

I shrugged. "It's been growing all day. I can't make it stop; not even spending time at the waterline soothed it. I've never felt something so intense."

I noticed a look of anticipation pass through Sarah's eyes, though whether it was good or bad was hard to tell. I hated that this urge to be somewhere else had become a concern. Truth be told, the sensation scared me, but it was also exciting. Something was close. Something that would change my world… I knew it, could feel it. I just had to find it.

Sarah looked to Amber, as usual, for guidance but my sister could only shrug.

"I got nothing."

Clara shuffled in my direction, staring at me with her watery blue eyes. "It's a sign. Middle Weaver senses the hunter, and the Goddess is telling her to flee." She grabbed my arm, her knobby hands surprisingly strong for such an old lady. "You must listen to the call, child. Run far away from here. The hunter will not spare you because of your youth. They prefer to kill while the witch is young, before her power of defense grows too strong. They'd kill all the witchlings if they could."

"We do have names, you know." Scarlett stepped between the old witch and me, Amber quickly joining her. No one threatened one of the Weaver girls without earning the wrath of the other two. We were often viewed as one entity instead of three grown women with minds of our own. Most of the time, this rankled, but when we were in trouble, the bond between us worked in our favor. There was no taking on one sister—if someone chose to attack one, they'd be dealing with all three.

"No one is running and no one is getting killed." Sarah glowered at the older witch until she released my arm. She then nodded at Bethesda, the current high priestess of the coven, before addressing the witches who'd gathered around us. "Amber doesn't sense a hunter, but Clara is convinced one is near due to the wolf she says was in our woods. I'm not disregarding the claim that danger could be close, only asking that we not overreact until we know more. We need confirmation that there's a hunter in our midst before we can direct the coven on what to do."

"One of us could be dead by the time we have confirmation he's a hunter," Clara's daughter called from her place beside her mother.

"No one is dying." Sarah stepped into the center of the circle, raising her voice and eyeing each woman in turn. She was the epitome of a powerful witch—long, white hair blowing in the wind, standing barefoot in the grass despite the cold to keep her connection to her power. Though not as strong or agile as she'd once been, she still commanded the attention of the witches. "The coven will stay put until we know more. Amber will meditate tonight to clear her sight. And tonight, I'll spend time with Clara and Bethesda in the ritual room to search the grimoire for references to witch hunters. If there's a threat, Bethesda will call a meeting of the elders to determine our best course of action. For now, I want everyone to settle down. There's no need to panic."

There was a great deal of whispers and mumbling as the members of the coven broke apart to return to their homes. Everyone was anxious, worrying about the extermination a witch hunter could do. It'd happened before, in other towns, and to other covens. Whole families wiped out in a blink, leaving no trace of them or their magick. So while Clara jumping to the conclusion that there was a hunter in the woods was a bit farfetched, it was still something to worry about. A witch hunter would murder us all without pause or regret. All because they believed witches worshiped the devil. Idiots…if they actually knew anything about us, they'd know we not only didn't worship the devil, we didn't even believe in one.

"Girls, let's go," Sarah mumbled, sounding more tired than she had just moments before. The cold weather had been wearing on her, and the shorter days due to the time change had us all a bit weary. We turned to head toward the lighthouse where we lived with a number of other coven witches, but Sarah stopped us.

"No, no, this isn't right." She shook her head and closed her eyes for a moment before glancing between the three of us. "Amber, go to the house for your meditation. We need to determine what's happening before we have a revolt from the rest of the coven. Azurine"—she met my anticipatory gaze with a small smile—"you need to run. Go south like you want to. Run until you find what it is your soul needs."

My heart raced at the thought of following the pull, but there were things to do, books and documents to study. I'd read and reread every book in the official coven library ever since I was a child; if there was information to be found, I'd be the best one to search for it.

"I should stay and help the coven." Even as I spoke the words, I tasted their wrongness. My soul didn't need to be in the ritual room, poring over old books and papers. It needed to be out, to answer the call it had been hearing all day. And luckily, Sarah seemed to know this and accept it before I did.

"The Fates are telling you to go south. I suggest you follow their guidance." Sarah gave me a small shrug. "Your intuition is strong, but mine is stronger. If you go south, I have a feeling something wonderful will come your way. Scarlett, go with her. Don't separate, and keep each other safe."

"But what if—" Amber's argument was cut off by Sarah's harsh cough. We all watched as her body seized and trembled with the effort, suffering right alongside her. When she was finished, Sarah shook her head.

"Trust the Fates, Amber Jane. They're calling to your sister for a reason." She turned toward the lighthouse, linking arms with Amber as they began the trek toward the old brick building lighting up the sky. "There's magick in the air tonight, Azurine. Don't miss the chance to experience it."

As they reached the stone pathway leading to the porch, I turned to Scarlett, still unsure about what I should do. Torn, really. To stay and help the coven research or go and find… something. But Scarlett could only shrug.

"She told you to go; we've never really disobeyed her before." She rolled her eyes at my raised eyebrows. "Not about magick type stuff."

My eyebrows went higher, making Scarlett huff.

"I did *not* set the porch on fire, so don't even bring that up." She looked over the grass around the lake, pulling her fleece jacket tighter around her and shivering in the cold night air. "We go home or we follow whatever bug's crawled up in your magick grill. You decide. But either way, I'd really like to get moving. It's cold out here."

I swallowed, nearly shaking with the need to run. This was it; my chance to discover what had been calling to me all day. Closing my eyes and giving myself over to the power within, I let the call of the water guide me to make my decision. Without conscious thought, I started running.

South.

My very soul sang as I finally headed in the right direction, happy and anxious to get to what was waiting for me. We ran down the beach, following the shore. Once we had traveled far enough to be outside the circle of light cast by the lighthouse, Scarlett moved to a position just slightly ahead of me. She led me toward the trees, flames burning bright on the ends of her fingers, lighting our way through the night. Though the moon was high and nearly full, it didn't filter through the trees set back off the coast. And that was where we needed to go. Into the woods.

The pull that had been tormenting me all day roared, a great wave of need making me run faster as I turned slightly off the path.

"Zuri! Where are we going?"

I ignored Scarlett and continued, surrendering to the need, heading exactly where my soul wanted to be. Over rocks and past trees, following the shoreline but veering farther and farther inland. As I came to a small creek, I turned west, following the water as it carved a road deeper into the woods. This continued for what had to be close to half a mile. South then west, south then west, mirroring the curve of the coast without running too near the water's edge. Scarlett stayed at my side, following my lead and lighting our way, but I couldn't focus on her. There was nothing but the want. Nothing but the pressure to be elsewhere. Nothing but—

I tried to stop as I raced into a clearing lit by a campfire, but the sudden change in ground and speed made me stumble. A second later, Scarlett crashed into me from behind, knocking us both to the ground. We scrambled to right ourselves, working against one another as we pushed and twisted.

"Damn it, hold still," Scarlett hissed. I huffed and stopped fighting, relieved when her weight finally left my body. As I lifted my face out of the dirt, ready to be humiliated by whoever had seen our fall, I was met with muddy gray fur, blindingly white teeth…

And the deep and terrifying growl of the huge wolf standing right in front of me.

THREE

WE ROLLED ONTO FERAL Breed land and parked next to Rebel's truck. My stomach dropped at the sight of the black Ford he drove when not on his bike. He'd given me a job to do. Well, a couple of jobs. Start investigating the issues at the Kalamazoo den and check in on his new bagger. I had nothing on the missing shifter yet except Beast's claim that Spook wasn't that type of guy, and we'd left Rebel's bike at the Yard Shark garage to bring mine to the camp. We should have left mine and brought the bagger, or I should have ridden over on the bike instead of in the truck. Either probably would have been a better decision.

The fire was already burning bright against the dark of the early nightfall. All four cabins were lit from within, bathing the area in a golden light, but the place might as well have been a haunted house for the anxiety rushing through my blood. I'd only just arrived, yet I felt as if I'd already failed.

"Looks like they got here a little earlier than planned." Beast nodded toward the stack of firewood against the shed on the far side of the property. Easily five feet high and fifteen feet long, the pile would've taken Rebel hours to chop. I should've been there to help him—just another failure to add to my list.

I grunted, swinging open the door and stepping out of Beast's truck. The two men had a thing for big, burly utility vehicles. Most of the guys from our den had one or two cars available for when the weather turned too cold to ride the bikes. Trucks, SUVs, muscle cars—when the days grew short and the wind turned wicked, they'd line the curb outside the denhouse. I rode my bike until the cold forced me to put it in storage, but I didn't own another vehicle. I couldn't see spending the money on a car I would hate to drive when I only needed it for a few months out of the year. Besides, no matter how much money I earned, an extra vehicle seemed extravagant. My feet or paws could get me to most of the places I needed to go if I couldn't take my bobber or hitch a ride with one of the guys from my den.

"Well, well, well, look what the cat dragged in."

Rebel stood on the porch of the second cabin wearing a pair of faded blue jeans and his black leather jacket. He looked… tired. Not in a good way, not like he'd been banging his mate all night and hadn't spared a single second to rest. More like something was weighing on his mind.

"Keep your pussy to yourself, old man." Beast bounded up the stairs and gave Rebel a rough slap on the back. "Congrats on your mating. I look forward to meeting her."

A muscle in Rebel's jaw tightened. "Yeah, I'm sure Charlotte will be out here any minute. C'mon, let's get closer to the fire. The temperature's dropping fast."

He glanced at me, eyes dark and face serious. I didn't duck my head, but I tilted it in a sign of submission. It must have been enough for the irritated shifter because he gave me a nod before heading for the fire pit.

As he walked away, I asked, "Where's Julian?"

My question stopped Rebel in his tracks. He turned slowly,

eyes burning with Alpha power as he looked my way. The weariness I'd noticed a few moments before was gone, replaced with a stoic façade the likes of which could rival even Gates.

"He's with friends for the week. Charlotte and I have a lot of things to talk about, and I figured the time alone would be good."

I nodded, my eyes darting to the door as the woman in question walked out. Tall, blond, with killer curves and sharp eyes, she'd make any man drop to his knees and beg for a little attention. But she was also smart and had a sarcastic sense of humor. Though there was no sign of her usual bright smile today. In fact, the woman looked like someone on the way to the gallows.

She eyed Beast from the porch, the scent of her adrenaline meeting my nose as her fear increased. Charlotte hadn't gotten the best introduction to wolf shifters, so I could understand her fear for the most part. But she knew me, and her mate was standing only a few feet away. Rebel would die to protect her, so there wasn't anything to be afraid of. And yet, her human heart raced to a beat I worried would send her into some kind of attack.

"Kitten." Rebel held out his hand. Charlotte eyed it then looked back over at Beast before refocusing on Rebel. She was terrified; I could smell it, sense it. I just wasn't sure why. But as she grew more frightened, and as her eyes darted from Rebel to Beast, I began to understand. Unfortunately, so did Beast.

"I'm not as ugly on the inside as I am on the outside, *conejita*. You can settle down." Beast glowered at the woman until Rebel stepped between the two. The tension rose as they stared, growls sounding in the cold evening air.

"I'm sorry." Charlotte's quiet voice broke the two from their staring contest as they both whipped their heads in her direction. She stood almost beside Rebel, remaining one step behind him as if afraid Beast would physically attack her. "I didn't mean to stare. I just—"

Beast didn't wait for her excuses. He spun on his heel and walked away, heading toward the tree line where the path to the lakefront began.

"I'm taking the last cabin. You all can figure out the rest of the accommodations without me."

I watched him leave, frustration a bitter burn on my tongue. The judgment Beast received due to his scars and his ink was something I'd long since grown used to witnessing, though I'd never expected one of the Feral Breed's own to be the one delivering it. And though Charlotte wasn't a member of the Breed, as a mate to one, I'd expected the same level of respect from her as I did from Rebel.

Charlotte clung to Rebel's side, looking as if someone had just kicked her puppy. "I didn't mean to upset him."

Rebel grabbed her and pulled her into his arms. "I know. Beast's just—"

The longer Rebel struggled with a descriptor for the man who'd introduced me to this new life, the angrier I became.

"Beast is Beast. Before you go pegging him with any other label, you might want to remember the definition of loyalty."

Rebel growled and turned to angle himself in front of Charlotte. As if he actually believed I would do anything to put her at risk. Rebel may have been my den president, a respected leader within the Feral Breed, but at that moment, I felt let down by him. His mating had truly knocked him off his game.

"You might want to watch your tongue, Pup. I don't yet see a Breed insignia on that leather coat."

"Don't." Charlotte pushed away from Rebel and took a step toward me. "It's my fault. Leaving my brother for the week and all the other stuff going on, it's got me on edge. Rebel's just…"

She glanced back at the man in question. His eyes met hers,

a look of something wary and dark crossing his face. Something was definitely off between them, though I had no desire to find out what. I just hoped they could figure it out. And soon.

I shrugged, my body practically itching to shift and run. "It's fine."

Charlotte turned my way, a small smile on her face. "It's not. I was rude, and Rebel defending me when I'd been completely in the wrong, while sweet, didn't help things. I'll apologize to Beast."

"You don't need to apologize," Rebel said.

"Yes, I do. And so do you." She gave him a serious look, one filled with hidden meaning. "If you're doing this, then we both have to figure out how to make it work. That means I have to get over my fear, and you have to figure out how to not always be the protective asshole I know so well. These are your brothers. We both need to treat them that way."

The two held each other's gaze for a few seconds before Rebel sighed and nodded.

"Fine." He leaned down and kissed the tip of her nose before meeting my gaze. If the look on his face was any indication, apologizing was the last thing he wanted to do. "My bad."

"Whatever, man. We're cool." I rolled my shoulders, cracking my neck. Something had the wolf inside me hyped up. Whether it was Rebel's odd behavior or knowing Beast had been hurt by Charlotte's reaction to him, I had no idea. It could've been neither. But the feeling of something coming, something big, wrapped itself around me and had me practically dancing in my need to shift. "I think I'm going to head out for a run."

Rebel's brows drew together. "You okay?"

As he waited on my response, his blue eyes seemed to travel over every inch of my body, looking for signs of danger. When they came back to meet mine, he watched me, practically stared straight into my soul to examine both the man and the wolf residing within. It took only a few seconds, the briefest of moments for my wolf to settle a bit under his gaze. There he was; the man who'd led me into more fights than I could count. Who'd looked me over in that same intensive way nearly every day since I'd started hanging around the Feral Breed den. The leader who loved his brothers and was hard on us in equal measure. I hadn't realized how much I'd missed that quintessential Rebel-inspection until I was the subject of it once more.

I calmed under his gaze, knowing my pack was coming back together after being apart for too long. "If you mean, do I think I'm going apeshit; no, I'm fine. I'm feeling sort of twitchy—maybe it's the coming full moon."

Rebel continued to stare at me, still in his concerned-leader role.

"I thought shifters weren't affected by the full moon," Charlotte said.

"They're not." Rebel gave me one more full review before he huffed. "As long as you're sure you're stable."

"Solid. As a rock." I pounded my chest twice, grinning when Rebel rolled his eyes. "Sorry for the smart comment, Charlotte. I've got a bit of a soft spot for the old man."

"No worries. I've got a bit of a soft spot for this old man as well." She pointed her thumb at Rebel. "The old ones really seem to know how to screw with your brain."

I chuckled as Rebel growled and lifted her into his arms. "Old man? I'll show you an old man."

I turned and left them to their mating haze. Whatever was happening between them—good or bad—they didn't need me witnessing it. I hoped Charlotte and Rebel would find time to settle things with Beast, if only because I knew how much being judged for his appearance bothered him. Not that he'd say the words. Beast was filled with as much testosterone and male pride as the rest of us. Admit a weakness? Never.

But I knew.

I hurried to the third cabin in the string, still feeling the need to go wolf and get a little exercise. I hadn't been exaggerating when I said something was making me twitchy. I had a sudden urge to shift, to run, to hunt for…something. I just didn't know what that something was.

Apparently, Beast felt the same as his black-as-pitch wolf form was already sitting on the steps to his cabin, his muzzle in the air.

"I swear, sometimes it's like you can read my mind."

Blue eyes met mine as he turned. He chuffed once, an irritated sound, then got to his feet and growled.

"Yeah, yeah. Give me a second. I don't want to mess up these jeans."

I ran inside the cabin next to Beast's and tossed my duffel bag on the bed. Within seconds, I was naked and staring down at myself. At my dick to be precise. I was hard. Not semi or chub-like hard, but fully and totally erect. For absolutely no reason. And every hair on my body was standing on end.

"What the fuck?"

I ran my fingers over the head of my penis and down to the base, but something didn't feel right. Which was damned ridiculous. My own hand should feel just fine. I'd been jerking myself off since I was twelve. My hand had long been my most reliable and consistent partner. Yet right then, as I tugged and swirled my thumb over the tip, the sensation felt foreign.

I huffed and thought about my options. I could jerk it— try to rub one out before heading for a run. But with the way my body was recoiling from my own touch, I doubted I'd be successful in anything other than giving myself a rash. Plus Beast was waiting, and he'd know exactly what I'd been doing if I wasn't outside in about six seconds. I could shift and hope it went down in the process. That had worked before when I'd been interrupted while in the company of a shewolf at the denhouse in K-zoo. Making your bones break and reform in the blink of an eye had a way of deflating an erection.

I opted for option two and prayed like hell that I didn't end up with a red lipstick boner between my legs when I hit four paws. Concentrating on the wolf within, I closed my eyes and gave myself over to the staticky feeling of shifting from one form to another. Once I'd wolfed up and shaken out my fur, I took a moment to just be, to really sink into my wolf instincts.

And then I whimpered.

My wolf spirit lunged inside of me, desperate and furious as the human side of my mind fought against him. The wolf wanted to run, to get out in the woods, to head north and not stop until…something. For the first time since those weeks after the attack and bite that had led me to my shifter life, the wolf inside of me exerted his individuality and tried to force the human side into submission. I grappled mentally with the beast, hanging on to my humanity by the barest thread. I couldn't last much longer against the need to run; it took nearly all of my energy to keep from bolting out the door and racing for whatever it was that was calling to me.

North north north north

I growled and planted my paws, stretching my claws until they dug deep into the wood floor. A responding growl had me bracing for attack, but it was only Beast in wolf form standing at the open door. His blue eyes met mine for a moment before sliding over the rest of me. I could picture what he had to be seeing—I was a back arched, claws out, panting mess of a wolf.

The pull grew stronger, demanding I move. I fought against the need, against the want of my wolf, but it was no use. A sharp mental yank had me surrendering. I took two running steps then jumped over Beast, sailing across the porch and landing on the dirt. As soon as my paws made contact, I was in motion. Running, racing, across camp and toward the north tree line. Something I needed was there. Something I had to have. Something that needed me just as much. Only I didn't know what it was.

I'd expected the wolf to completely take over our joint mind, but I kept my human thoughts in place. I knew who I was and what was waiting for me in camp, but the wolf disregarded it all. His focus was one hundred percent on the woods to the north, where the night had fallen a little faster due to the tall trees, and the shadows both invited me in and warned me away in turn. Something was in those woods. Something important.

Before I could reach the trees, Beast slammed into me, knocking into my flank hard enough that I fell to the side and slid on my hip. I hurried to my feet and spun, snarling. He didn't understand, didn't know how desperate my inner wolf was to move. I had to go north.

Beast circled, stepping between me and where I needed to be. My snarl turned vicious, the fur along my nape standing on end as I readied for a fight. Beast matched me in volume and aggression, his snarl turning to deep, grunting barks as he threatened me.

"What the fuck?" Rebel hurried over, his stride long and his eyes hard. "I don't know what the problem is here, but it needs to end now. Shift back."

I bared my teeth as the man whose orders I was trained to follow demanded I do the exact opposite what I knew I should. Rebel stared at me, waiting for me to comply, but my wolf refused to submit. Not this time.

When I didn't drop my stare or give in to his demand, he raised his voice.

"Pup, you will shift back now."

The weight of the Alpha order was like a lead blanket being

draped across my shoulders. My wolf and I fought against it, our growl deepening. We could not risk giving in, could not stop until we'd reached whatever it was that called to us in those woods.

North north north north

Beast shifted to his human form and hurried to Rebel's side.

"What the hell is wrong with him?"

Rebel shook his head. "No clue, but he said he was feeling a little off."

"Well, this is a fuckton more than just a little off."

I spun and faced north as the scent of two humans met me. No, not humans. Something…other. Something my wolf recognized but my human side didn't. The one scent made me want to attack, to protect my den and my pack from the unknown threat. But the other…

Deep and sweet, the smell was like waking up on the riverbank as a kid with the mist rolling over the water and the sun playing hopscotch across the ripples and waves. It was like home and faith and all the good things I'd long ago had taken from me. It was everything…and it was mine.

"What the hell is that?" Beast turned toward the tree line just as two women burst through the brush and out of the shadows. They stumbled and fell, toppling over each other and landing in a heap. Beast growled and stepped in their direction, but my wolf howled in my head and forced us to intervene. Without thought or intention, I jumped past the man I saw as my most trusted brother, my maker, and turned on him. Three barks had him stepping back.

"Easy, Pup. I'm not going to hurt them." Beast put his hands up and took another step back, pulling Rebel with him. Their retreat settled my inner wolf enough to back up, to move closer to the women who were still lying on the ground. Once I stood beside them, I dared to turn my face away from the threats in front of us, the human side of me needing to know why my wolf was adamant we protect the women. I continued to growl lowly as I looked over the pile of girl-flesh, the human side winning back more and more control as the seconds passed.

And when the girl on the bottom looked up, when her sea green eyes met mine, I knew I'd never be the same again. My wolf settled, allowing my human side full control of my body and my thoughts. Which was good, because if the way my heart drew me toward the unknown woman was any indication, I'd found my mate.

And she looked terrified.

FOUR

Azurine

PAWS, CLAWS, FUR, TEETH…*hunter.*

I struggled to my knees, scared the wolf could attack at any moment. His growls filled the air, sending chills up and down my spine. Scarlett gasped beside me, obviously seeing the same thing I did. I trembled as I moved back, lifting my head as the growls grew louder, certain the pain of teeth slicing into my flesh was coming.

Instead, I met pale green eyes. Intelligent, caring, and inquisitive eyes that showed far too much depth to belong in the face of an animal. They made me pause, made the fear of my initial reaction recede. The wolf's very presence should have terrified me. Should have had me running the other way and shouting for help, but those eyes calmed me.

As soon as our gazes locked, an incredible sense of peace washed through me, cool and calm. This was where I was meant to be. The wolf was what had been calling to me all day, though how or why I still had no idea. But there was one thing I was absolutely sure of: if there was a witch hunter in these woods, the wolf before me was not him.

The wolf took a single step closer, just one paw, but it was enough for my sister to see him as a threat.

"Zuri…stay down!"

Before I could react, a ball of flames erupted between the wolf and me, sending sparks and ash into the air and making him retreat.

"No!" I hurried to my feet and tried to grab Scarlett so she wouldn't attack again, but it was too late. Two fireballs went screaming in the direction of my wolf.

As I spun to see the damage she'd caused, a man grabbed Scarlett and lifted her off the ground with his arm around her neck. Fury raged through me, pure anger at the audacity of the stranger to put his hands on my sister. Without pause, I called my power through me, chanting to the elements in my mind. This was no time to be shy, and I was no scared little witch afraid of being burned at the stake. I'd drop a tsunami on his ass if he attempted to hurt my sister.

With the full power of the magick of the water within me, I spread my fingers and turned my palms skyward. Almost instantly, the winds picked up around me, going from a simple breeze to a howling gust. The man holding Scarlett took a step back, fear burning in his eyes as hail the size of golf balls began to fall on his head. Scar's fingers glowed against the skin of his arm where it held her throat, a sign she was still drawing on her beloved fire element. But he didn't pull away from her fiery touch, which really pissed me off. My wolf made a sound like a whine from behind me, but I couldn't lose my focus. My sister was in danger, and I had to protect her.

Feet planted, hands out, I looked the scarred man right in the eye and smiled. Then I puckered my lips and blew.

A mass of air exploded between us, screaming in a banshee wail as the moisture from my breath expanded and formed a large wave. The man's face paled, his eyes nearly bugging out of his head as a wall of water built between us. Ten feet tall and six feet across, it was a physical force one could feel and see as it glittered in the firelight. I directed the wall toward the man with my fingertips, forcing him backward another step or two before he started growling.

"Your little magic tricks don't scare me, witch." He glared, still a tad pale. But the fear on his face was quickly morphing into fury. When I took another step toward him, he tightened his hold on Scarlett. Sparks flew from her fingers, but her eyes were bulging and she obviously couldn't breathe. There'd be no way to magick her way out of his grasp if she panicked, and that was exactly what it looked like she was doing.

I scowled, hoping to hide the growing sense of panic that I wouldn't be able to help my sister, before raising my right hand, making the wave grow from ten feet to fifteen on one side. The man watched warily as I bent the top of the wall over his head. When I had him covered, his face began to transform, small black dots of what looked like fur pushing through the skin. It was disconcerting at best and terrifying at worst, but I couldn't show fear. The bastard had his forearm pressed against Scarlett's throat as if to suffocate her. There was no time for fear.

"Let her go, you freak. You don't want to cross us." I did my best to portray the calm and collected witch, but inside I was scrambling.

He tightened his hold on Scarlett with a wicked grin. Her eyes bulged as she gripped his arm, obviously having trouble breathing under the pressure. A deep growl came from behind me, from the wolf I saw as mine, but I had to ignore him. I'd been trained since birth to do no harm, and yet this man before me, this animal, had my sister in a choke hold. While the coven would be forced to punish me should I cross the line from defensive spellcasting to offensive, I had to consider that this man could be a witch hunter and therefore a serious danger to me and my sister. I was running out of time.

"Let her go!" I flung my arms to the side and called the power of the waves to protect my sister. With little effort, I directed the flow of water in an arc so debris from the forest floor caught in the churning, gravity-defying wave. Sticks and leaves floated between us, whipping this way and that in the wall of water. "Let my sister go, or by the Goddess, I will drown you where you stand."

The man growled louder. "You'll have to go through her to get to me. Seems counterproductive if you're trying to protect the fire-bitch."

Before I could answer, my wolf stalked in front of me, head lowered and lips curled back in a snarl. The man holding Scarlett looked surprised for a second before his eyes went to something over my shoulder. Without warning, thick arms wrapped around my neck and waist, yanking me off my feet. The wall I'd been controlling released with a boom, thundering through the air as water and forest debris fell to the ground, creating a muddy, mucky mess. I tried to fight off the person behind me, even managed a small scream, but they were too strong and too fast. My wolf, responding to my cut-off scream, spun. He released a snarl that sent a shiver of icy fear up my spine as he dropped his head and stalked closer.

"Pup, no," the man holding Scarlett screamed to my wolf, but it was too late. Without warning, the animal jumped, his teeth coming down on the arm at my waist and instantly drawing blood.

"Fuck, Pup." The hold around me loosened for a moment, but it was enough time for me to drop my head and bite the arm that had been around my neck. My captor didn't release me, but he did take a step back and curse, causing my wolf to release his lower arm.

"Damn it, quit fucking biting me, you two. What's going—"

A loud whistle sounded, making all of us turn. A pretty

woman with long, blond hair stood on the other side of the campfire, her hip cocked and a single brow raised.

"What the hell is wrong with you guys? Quit behaving like animals and let those women go."

The man holding Scarlett growled. "This doesn't concern you, *conejita*."

My captor pulled me to the side, which caused my wolf to increase the volume of his snarl and circle as if to attack again.

"Oh, for fuck's sake." The woman approached, seemingly unafraid. "These boys are a little overzealous at times, but they mean well. I'm pretty sure the little firestarter act made them a bit nervous."

"Charlotte." The man holding me sounded a warning.

"Abraham." She shot back, sarcasm obvious in her tone. "Don't even think about trying to tell me to back off. I'm not some delicate porcelain doll with no common sense. I saw what happened, and you two are seriously in the wrong on this one."

She stepped forward, brushing past my wolf and patting him on the head. It probably wouldn't have seemed like such an odd gesture had the giant animal not still been growling at the man behind me. Teeth bared, drool spraying as the rumble ripped from his chest, he looked fierce and ready to kill. Yet the woman acted as if that was a normal, everyday occurrence. A house pet in the skin of a wild animal.

She finally stopped directly in front of the man holding my sister, though she directed her words to the captive, not the captor.

"I know you were protecting the other girl, but I can assure you there was no need. None of us means you any harm. If I promise no danger will come to you two, will you promise not to set things on fire until we can at least figure out what the hell is going on?"

Scarlett met my gaze. I gave her as much of a nod as I could considering I was still being restrained. The soft fur of the wolf at my feet brushed against the front of my legs, reinforcing my opinion that we would be safe here. He wouldn't let anything happen to us. How I knew that he was a he and that he would keep his friends in check, I had no clue. I just did. He was no danger to me.

Scarlett grimaced for a moment before croaking out a "Deal."

"Awesome. Now you." She came to stand in front of me. "Something's got Pup all worked up, and I'm pretty sure I know what it is. Promise not to try to drown us all if I make these Neanderthals keep their hands off you two?"

I glanced down at my wolf. "Sounds like a plan."

She looked over my shoulder to the man holding me.

"Let her go, now. That means you too, Beast."

"They're witches," the guy holding Scarlett practically hissed. "You can't trust them."

The woman cocked her head and spun. "And you boys are wolf shifters who tried to choke them into submission for doing nothing but running into our campsite. Pah-tay-toe, pah-tah-toe." She stepped closer, the man behind me growling low and threatening as she walked right up to the one she called Beast. "Sometimes you have to take people on faith instead of making assumptions about them. I was wrong about you, and you're wrong about them. I know it."

Beast stared at her for a moment before looking at the man over my shoulder with a scowl. "Are we supposed to take orders from your—"

"Do it."

The voice from behind me was strong, leaving no room for disagreement. Beast glared over my shoulder before finally dropping his arms from around Scarlett. She fell to her knees, clutching her throat and coughing. As soon as the man let me go, I rushed over to kneel beside my sister.

"You okay?"

She nodded then looked over my shoulder. "Uh, Zuri?"

I felt the wolf come closer before she spoke, knew he was there by the way my heart sang for him. His warmth and the aura of positive energy around him made me hyperaware of his presence.

"It's okay. He's kind of mine."

Mine. Such an odd thing to be so sure about. But I felt the connection that joined me to the animal, and though new and strange, refused to deny it.

I turned and met the pale green eyes of the wolf I'd been drawn to, my heart thumping faster as the link between us burned hot and bright. He licked his lips and lowered himself to the ground, never breaking eye contact.

I crawled closer, pushing off Scarlett's hand when she grabbed for me. I knew what she'd say, how she'd warn me against getting closer to what she assumed was either a dangerous animal or a werewolf sent to destroy our coven. But I saw the soul in his eyes; I knew there was more to him than the fur and paws of his current form. And I was positive he was no hunter.

"Charlotte said your friends were wolf shifters. Should I assume you are as well?"

The wolf whined and settled his head on his paws.

"I think that's a yes." Scarlett knelt beside me, both of us watching as the wolf huffed. He sat up, his head lifting a few times as his tongue again appeared to lick the length of his snout.

Charlotte giggled from where she stood with a muscled blond man. "It's like animal charades. Shift back, Pup. Make this whole thing easier on the girl."

The wolf chuffed in her direction before turning back to meet my gaze. Unable to resist, I reached to stroke his ears. His head dropped and he made a sound that was half whine, half growl.

"Don't get me wrong, I'm an animal lover by nature." I ran my fingers to the tips of his ears, squeezing the pressure point there before sliding back down. Soft and warm, they felt like velvet under my fingertips. "You're quite a handsome wolf, but talking to me would be easier in your human body. Can you go human for me, please?"

Scarlett and I stood as the wolf hopped to his paws. Within seconds, a man stood before me where once my wolf had been. Tall and fair with a mess of wavy blond hair, he towered over me in a way that made me feel safe instead of scared. Big arms, a broad chest, flat stomach, muscled thighs. California-beach-boy handsome. And all of him naked. Very, very naked.

"Are you okay?" he asked, his eyes running up and down my body as he seemed to inspect me for some unknown damage.

"I'm fine. No blood, no foul."

His eyes met mine and his plump, pink lips curved into a delicious smile, one that made my heart race and my legs quiver.

"Hi." His simple greeting was intriguing and adorable.

"Hi," I replied with a smile of my own.

"So we have a new mate to add to the party, is that what's happening here?" Charlotte glanced between the man in front of me and the one who'd captured me earlier.

"Pup, is that what's going on?" the man who was not Beast asked.

Pup nodded, his eyes never leaving mine. "Sure looks like it."

I grinned as his aura cleared, finally able to see why I felt so attracted to him. "You have my red thread wrapped around you."

His face scrunched into a confused look that made me giggle.

I took a step in his direction, wanting to touch him, to feel the connection smoldering in my body ignite. Unfortunately, my sister wasn't quite convinced.

"Hold up." Scarlett grabbed my arm and pulled me back. "What's wrong with you? First of all, red thread? You're really going to buy that shit? No one's found their so-called red thread in hundreds of years. They don't exist. Also, in case you've forgotten, these guys are werewolves…as in men who turn into wolves…as in the hounds of Hell. Witch hunters."

"We're not witch hunters." Pup stepped forward, his hand brushing against my wrist, making us both shiver. "And we're wolf shifters, not werewolves."

"What's the difference?" Scarlett looked pissed and not at all ready to believe a word Pup said.

The other man, the one I had to assume was Abraham, took a step toward us. "Shifters have control of themselves when they change form. We change at will, not because of the lunar cycle. And we don't kill people."

Charlotte coughed, causing Abraham's mouth to turn down in a frown.

"We don't kill people…unless they deserve it."

Scarlett rolled her eyes. "Well, that's comforting. Hope we don't end up deserving to be dinner."

"We don't eat people, and we don't hunt witches. That's a totally different class of fucked up." The man they called Beast walked past us. "Only you would find your mate in a witch, Pup. And, by the way, you might want to cover your junk."

Pup jerked, bringing his hands in front of him in a show of modesty that made me giggle. Not that I hadn't already gotten an eyeful.

"Sorry. I didn't think about the fact that I was naked."

I smiled. "I didn't mind."

Pup's eyes traveled down my body and back up again, his

interest apparent. "So…red thread?"

"Yup. Wrapped all around you."

He nodded, a smile growing on lips so pink, they looked painted. "Chinese folklore, right? Destined lovers, sort of like our"—he licked his lips as his smile grew—"soul mates."

"Exactly." I grinned at him, all wide and cheesy. Red threads, soul mates, fated mates, destined lovers; whatever legend or title I chose to apply, he was mine. The other half to my soul. The man made for me by the Fates.

Scarlett huffed. "The coven's going to blow a gasket."

"They can do whatever they like." I turned to glare at her. "The thread of my soul led me here, to him. I'm not going to ignore the call, and I'm not going to think less of him and his friends because they're not fully human. Neither are we, if you remember correctly."

"Whatever. You chill out with your new pet. I'll be making a s'more." She stalked off toward what had been the fire in the center of the clearing, now nothing more than a smoking stack of burnt logs. "You got any marshmallows, Char?"

"Of course," Charlotte said as she turned to the blond man standing next to her. "Can you get the fire going again?"

Scarlett smirked. "Yeah, that won't be a problem."

She grabbed an armful of logs from the stack next to the fire pit and tossed them on the smoldering pile in the pit. As sparks danced in the night sky, her fingertips glowed. Charlotte stared, her mouth falling open as flames erupted from my sister's hands. With a flick of her wrist, Scarlett threw a small fireball at the stack of wood in the fire pit, lighting a roaring fire in seconds. No one moved. The people around us stood and stared into the flames as if they'd never seen a fire before. I tried not to smile, but a grin crept across my face. I could make waves dance and ice form out of nothing but the moisture in the air, but Scarlett's fireballs were a scene-stealer.

"So, those marshmallows?" Scarlett dropped into a chair and pulled out her phone.

Charlotte nodded, still staring at the fire. "Sure. Okay."

After a few seconds of stunned silence, she and the blond man walked off, Beast having already disappeared into one of the cabins.

"I should go get some clothes on, and then maybe we can talk." Pup ducked his head, still blocking my view with his hands.

"I could come with you," I said, my voice a bit deeper than I'd expected. Pup's head popped up, his eyes a fiery jade as they met mine.

"You could, if you don't mind being alone with me."

"Sure, you don't scare me." I shrugged, trying to pull off casual. But deep down, I was anything but casual. I was excited and anxious, wanting so much to get this man alone so I could explore our bond. The emotional tie to him was already present, growing slowly tighter as it bound us together, but the physical one was burning hot and bright. A connection that made me want to strip off my clothes and offer myself to him to use in whatever way pleased him. And whatever way would please me as well.

Pup dropped his arms from in front of his body and held out a hand to me.

"I'm no threat to you." His words were a promise, one I was more than willing to put my faith in. I grinned as I took his offered hand, eyeing him in the process.

Pup walked with me to a small wooden cabin. "I'm in this one."

I bit my lip as we climbed the handful of stairs, surreptitiously watching the way the muscles in his thighs bulged with each step. When we reached the porch, he sort of hopped in front of me. I had to fight back a moan as I watched the muscles in his back and ass flex with the movements. He was so gorgeous, so strong and masculine. Tempting.

And I was about to be alone with him.

FIVE

I RAN MY HAND through my hair, cupping my junk with the other. This was insane. Of course I'd meet my mate while working. Of course I'd end up scaring the hell out of her. Of course she'd see me naked long before I planned on getting naked with her. And now I had to walk her inside the cabin, flashing my ass and my balls along the way.

Totally insane.

"I'm in this one." I directed her to the cabin I'd claimed as mine. She led the way up the stairs, her jeans pulling tight around her round ass as she stepped onto the porch. The swing of her hips captivated me, pulled all my focus, and made me miss the top step on my way up. She didn't seem to notice though, so I played it off as trying to step in front of her and lead her across the porch.

I opened the door for her when I reached it, my breaths coming quickly as I played every nasty, disgusting sex-ed picture from high school in my memory to keep my dick from getting any harder than it already was. She was so beautiful, so ridiculously sexy. From her long, dark hair to her deeply tanned skin, she was a darker version of an actress from another era.

Sensual and voluptuous.

She stopped just inside the door, forcing me to brush against her as I passed. Touching her, even so innocently, was like falling into a pit of pillows and blankets. Warm, comforting, and so damned soft.

Her face scrunched adorably as she looked over the rustic interior. I knew it wasn't much, but it was the Breed's place to hang while we were working on the western side of the state. And occasionally have a vacation.

But that opinion was my own. I suddenly had a mate, a female, who was probably used to more comfortable surroundings than a little cabin with plywood walls. My ears burned as I watched her eyes dance over the bed, the table, and finally the door to the simple bathroom.

"Sorry. It's a little—"

"It's fine." Her eyes met mine, her pouty lips tugging up into a smile. "There's a good energy here. Very calming. I like it."

I nodded, still unsure and feeling somehow inadequate. "Sure. Okay, I'm just going to—"

I pointed toward the duffel bag lying on the bed. Without waiting for a response, I hurried over and pulled out a pair of basketball shorts.

"So tell me, Pup," she said as I slid the fabric up my legs. "What do you do when you're not growling at women?"

I snorted a laugh, much more comfortable once my bare ass was covered. "For the record"—I yanked a T-shirt over my head—"I wasn't growling at you. More for you."

I turned, catching her staring at me in a decidedly lower location than my face. My lips tugged up into a smirk as her eyes finally met mine. She didn't look away or show any sign of embarrassment, just peered at me with those gorgeous green eyes, so much like the color of the lake on a cloudy day.

"Growling for me?"

Lowering my voice, I took two steps closer to her. "I knew you were my mate the second I saw you. Any growling after that point was definitely in defense of you."

Her eyebrows went up and she inched closer. "Oh, really?"

"Yes, really." Another step, putting me mere inches away from her.

"And what about my sister?"

"What *about* your sister?" I could feel her heat, smell her unique scent on the air. Jesus, I wanted to drink her in.

"Were you defending her as well?" She slid closer, her body barely brushing mine. Electricity. That was what touching her was like. Sparking blue and white bands of electricity joining us together.

I swallowed hard, entranced by those lips of hers. "Did you want me to?"

She shook her head, all slow and with a smile curving up her lips. I wanted to taste them so bad.

"No."

Her whisper made me tilt my head. "No?"

She brushed her hand against mine as she gazed at me, making me once again think of electricity, this time of lightning touching down. Making the earth shake with the power of its strike.

"No." Her voice was quiet, her words just for the two of us. "I kind of like the idea of you growling only for me."

I growled intentionally, low and deep as I stared down at her. "Like this?"

She slid closer, the way her tits pressed against my chest making me want to feel how soft she was everywhere else. As she edged into my space, my dick found a happy home trapped between us, pressing into her stomach. He liked it there, and there was no way she couldn't feel how much.

"Is that for me?"

I bit back a smile, wondering if she was implying more than just my growl. "Just for you."

She hummed and licked her lips, nearly sending me into cardiac arrest.

"Good. I prefer to keep some things to myself." Her grin was killer, stunning me with her beauty and making my breath catch. This girl. She made me want to throw her down on the floor and bury myself in her. Made me want to lick every inch of her skin. But we had this sexy, standing, getting-to-know-you thing going on, even if all I was learning was how turned on the woman could make me without even trying.

Daring to take things a step further, I placed one hand on her hip and pulled her even closer. She responded with a smile, not at all resistant to my hold.

"So apparently you don't play well with others." I grinned as she rolled her eyes. "And you make water appear out of nowhere. What more do I need to know? What do you do when you're not running through the forest like your ass is on fire?"

She smiled for a brief moment, but then her eyes grew wide and her mouth fell open. "Oh, hell, I almost forgot." She patted her pockets and, for some reason, grabbed her tits. Not that I minded watching her grope herself. Whatever she was looking for must not have been where she thought it should be, though. After coming up empty-handed, she looked around the room, obviously agitated.

"Do you have a phone?"

I grabbed my cell off the table and tossed it to her, immediately missing the physical connection we'd been sharing. She typed in some numbers before bringing the black device to her ear. I knew the second the phone was answered by the way her eyes closed in what looked like relief.

"Is everything okay?" She paced the room, eating up the space with her long stride. I sat on the edge of the bed, watching her. I couldn't keep my eyes off her. Long, black hair, golden skin, ripe, full body. And her walk, my god. Tits jiggling under her sweatshirt, hips swinging in those tight jeans—she gave me a show with every step. The way she moved was intoxicating.

"No, we're fine. How's Sarah? Did they find anything?" She paused and looked out the window, her face growing dark. "Don't listen to Scarlett. She's cranky and being a brat. We're okay, but some things have come up so we're probably going to hang here for a bit."

I raised an eyebrow and mouthed the word probably as she turned my way. She raised one right back and nodded, still talking on the phone.

"So Sarah's okay? Yeah, no. Don't wake her if she's sleeping. I'm fine; Scar's fine. There's no need to worry about us. We're safe here."

Her second eyebrow rose to match the first, as if looking for my agreement. I nodded, not sure what she would be worried about, but knowing, whatever it was, I'd take care of it. My mate would be safe with me no matter what.

The instinct to protect what was mine was a strong one, and something I wasn't completely prepared for. I'd seen it with Rebel and Gates, but this was different. It felt stronger than what I expected. Protecting this woman had instantly become the only thing in the world that held any importance to me, and that feeling scared the shit out of me.

I'd failed once when someone had been put in my care. I'd die if I failed again.

"I know." My mate sighed and sat down on the corner of the bed, still holding the phone to her ear. "Just get some sleep. We'll be home when we can. We can start again in the morning. Yeah, love you too."

My lips rose, baring my teeth in an almost unconscious show of irritation. I hated that she was telling someone else she loved them when I couldn't even reach out to hold her hand without second-guessing myself. But when I saw the way she was clutching my phone to her chest with her head bowed, I had to brush off my petty selfishness. This girl was in pain about something.

"Is everything okay?"

Her head whipped up at my voice, as if she'd forgotten I was in the room. "Yeah, it's just…"

I waited as she seemed to fight back some kind of strong emotion, looking both lost and angry. Her expressions made me want to comfort her and fight for her, though I had no idea which was needed. The inability to jump in and help her fix whatever was bothering her drove me mad. Just one more thing I couldn't get right, it seemed.

As she sat and stared at nothing, a warm draft blew through the cabin. Humidity. It was becoming extremely humid in the little cabin, making the hairs on my arms stand up as the window fogged over.

"Uh, are you doing that?" I nodded my head in the direction of the steamy windowpane when she looked up. She stared at me for a moment, as if unsure who I was or what I was talking about, but then she followed my gaze. Her mouth turned down into a frown when she saw the now opaque glass.

"Sorry." She took a deep breath and shook her head. "It's been a really weird night."

"Yeah." I leaned over my thighs and ran a hand over my face. "I can't imagine I'm helping much in the weird department."

She smiled, tilting her head to the side a little. "You're the most interesting thing that's happened to me in a long time."

My eyes met hers, a smile growing on my face. "Yeah?"

She stood and strolled over, not stopping until she was

standing between my thighs, her breasts at my eye level.

"Totally. And I'm a witch…interesting things happen to me all the time."

I wrapped my arms around her, loving how perfect she felt in my hold. As if made for me. As if her body pressed against mine was exactly where she should be. And deep down, I truly believed it was.

"So you really are a…witch." I hadn't meant to stumble over the last word, but it was hard to imagine true witches with powers and shit just running around the dunes of Lake Michigan. I wanted to kick myself for being so-not-smooth as her smile fell.

"Yes," she deadpanned. "And you're really a man who can morph into an overgrown dog."

"Wolf."

She shrugged. "Same difference."

I stood, towering over her, releasing a low growl as I caged her in with my body. "No. Not the same difference. A dog is a pet. A wolf is owned by no one."

I walked her backward until I had her pressed against the wall, breathing in the scent of her, desperate to feel more of her warmth against me. "A wolf values family, fights on behalf of his pack, lives by a hierarchy based on trust and respect." I paused, making sure I had her full attention before dropping my head to whisper in her ear. "And wolves mate for life."

She stood her ground, those lips turning up a bit as she peered up at me. "Mates for life, huh? Too bad I'm not able to get all furry with you."

"You don't need to." I reached for her hand, wrapping my fingers around hers and pulling our joined hands between us. I set the back of her hand against my chest, right over my racing heart, and massaged the side with my thumb. I held on to her lightly, just enough to ease the ache I felt around her, not pushing for anything more than simple contact. "We don't have to mate with one of our own. Shifters and humans end up together all the time."

She licked her lips, her eyes soft and wide. "Really? But what about witches and shifters? Because I'm not quite human."

I pressed myself against her, shivering when her body met the length of mine. "Neither am I. That doesn't mean we can't be…this."

She sighed, her free hand moving up my arm and around my neck. "This?"

"Yeah, this. Not love, not marriage, not anything demanding." I shrugged. "Just this, mates and strings."

She gave me a bit of an irritated look. "Threads, not strings."

"Threads." I leaned down to place a soft kiss on the tip of her nose. "Sorry."

Her smile spread like a sunrise—slow and bright—filling me with a sense of renewal, rebirth, and completion. This was my mate. My one. Rebel had waited two centuries to find Charlotte; Gates had waited four. I'd been a shifter for only ten years and had already been blessed with her presence. I was so fucking lucky.

"We can label it later." I kissed her nose again then leaned down to catch the corner of her mouth. A tiny kiss, barely a tease, but enough to set my world on fire. "For now, it's just this. A wolf and his witch."

"I like that." Her whispered response had me straining to keep my mouth off hers. Damn, I wanted her. Wanted every single piece of her. Wanted to never leave her side, to see every expression she could make, know every memory she had. She was mine…and I wanted to be hers as well.

When she yawned, I shook myself out of my mate-haze. It was late, and the poor girl had to be tired. I still had no idea what had sent her running through the woods, though I was glad for whatever it was. Good or bad, it had led her to me. I would forever be grateful.

Knowing we could do more talking if I made her a comfortable place to rest, I quickly grabbed the quilt off the bed and tossed it on the floor, adding a few pillows as well. And then I shrugged a single shoulder at her inquisitive look.

"I don't have a couch, and sitting on the bed seems presumptuous."

She grinned and lowered herself to the makeshift pallet, curling her legs underneath her. I followed her lead, edging close so I could bask in her scent and warmth as we sat on a sea of fabric.

"So." She leaned back, bracing her arms against the floor. "I guess we're both a little off the norm."

"Yep. Sure seems that way."

"But your off is different than my off." She huffed and shook her head. "I think we're screwed."

"Jesus, I hope so." I grinned as she cocked her head and gave me a look. It was a look I could remember receiving a lot in the past. The one that said "smartass" without actually saying the word.

She glanced around the room again, looking thoughtful. "You're a wolf shifter—you protect your breed, so you're kind of like a cop, and you're staying here but don't live here. I guess the next big thing that I don't know is your name. Unless Pup is a popular first name among the shifter set."

I grunted and glanced away, suddenly nervous. "It's Adam."

As I knew she would, she asked the one question I had no clue how to answer. "Adam what? What's your last name?"

I took a deep breath and stared at the floor. "I don't remember my full name."

The weight of the silence following that admission was worse than any I'd lived through before. But when she did speak, when she asked me the question I expected, her voice wasn't doubtful or pitying. It was calm, clear, and left me with no doubt that she truly wanted to know the answer.

"What do you mean, you don't remember your full name?"

I brought my gaze to meet hers, drowning in her almond-shaped eyes. "I was attacked by a shifter nomad, which was the reason I was turned. When I came back to my humanity after receiving my wolf spirit, my memories were foggy."

Her eyebrows drew together. "Is that normal? I mean, do all of you forget who you were?"

"No. Many of the shifters are born this way, born into a pack of their own. Even the ones who are turned like me normally remember their human memories. But my turning was pretty ugly. The memories disappeared."

"I can't imagine not remembering my aunt or my sisters." She closed her eyes and shook her head. "It would break my heart."

I linked my pinkie with hers, offering a quiet, subtle support. "I remember my mom. I remember being a gangly, awkward kid who fell down a lot. I remember how poor we were and meeting the man who would eventually introduce me to this life. I have memories, just not ones where someone calls me by my full name. Beast knows it but doesn't tell me because he thinks there's a reason for the block. So I'm Adam. But my Breed brothers call me Pup because I'm not a true member yet. I'm a prospect, working my way up to earn a patch and a road name."

She nodded, silent. I hated that my crappy memory had made her look even the tiniest bit unhappy. There was no need to be; I'd gotten over the holes in my memory years ago. They didn't bother me anymore, and I had no desire to search out information to questions that didn't need answers.

Wanting her attention back, I nudged her knee with my

own. "Tell me about yourself."

She shrugged. "Not much to tell. I'm one of the Weaver sisters. Middle one, to—"

"No."

She froze, staring at me in shock.

"Not your sisters. You. I want to know about you."

She seemed confused, as if I'd just demanded something she didn't know how to supply. I didn't want her to misunderstand me, so I grasped her hand and leaned closer.

"What's your name, pretty girl? Tell me about you. Just you."

She continued to stare at me for a few seconds, as if needing time to formulate an answer. But then she took a deep breath and smiled.

"My name is Azurine Weaver, and I'm a witch. My coven owns the old lighthouse up by Lake Parity."

I grinned, completely focused on my mate as she gave me bits and pieces of herself. "And what do you like to do in your spare time?"

She bit her lip, her eyes dancing around the room as she appeared to really give her answer some thought.

"I like to swim, of course. And I like to dance to cheesy pop music, but my sisters make fun of me for it so I tend to only do that when I know I can be alone. I hate to garden, but we have to dig in the dirt a lot because of all the plants we need for spells and tinctures. My coven thinks I'm crazy, but I can't stand the feeling of my hands being dirty. I prefer the winter to the summer, am a night owl and not a morning person, and have a huge coffee addiction that I refuse to relinquish. And I have a small obsession with fast cars and big motors."

I chuckled.

"What?" Her smile grew as she cocked her head.

"You're a little gearhead. What do you drive?"

She bit her lip, looking more adorable than I could have ever imagined. "I think I'll keep that one to myself. Make you work for it later."

I raised my eyebrows at her, making her laugh. The sound was beautiful and perfect, something I wanted to hear from her over and over and over again. Wanted to make it bigger and bolder, watch her give herself over to her happiness. I was turning into such a sap for this girl, not that I minded.

"What about you?" She inched closer, her eyes bright. "Tell me about you."

I straightened my back and held out my hand, taking hers in mine as if I were going to shake it.

"My name is Pup of the Feral Breed." I kissed the back of her hand, letting my lips brush gently across her soft skin. "I'm a wolf shifter who likes long walks on the beach, strawberries with my champagne, and a good scratch behind the ears now and again."

She laughed, throwing her head back. That was it—what I'd been waiting for. A laugh so strong, she didn't try to hold back. I loved it; loved the freedom with which she reacted to me in that moment. That was my Azurine, my mate, being her true self. And it was hotter than all the sultry looks and teasing glances could have ever been.

As her laughter slowed and she dropped her chin, her face turned a bit more serious. She licked her lips, her voice a rough whisper when she said, "The Fates picked you as my soul mate, tied a red thread between the two of us when we were still dancing in the Summerlands."

I rolled to my knees and crawled forward, each movement slow and precise. I didn't want to scare her but I had to be closer. I needed her near me, against me.

"The Fates picked you as my mate, my one need, the woman I will love and desire for the rest of my very long life."

Our eyes locked, the moment heavy. A breeze blew through the cabin, bringing a feeling of brightness with it. Like the wind right before the rain begins to fall, cool and soft with a tease of water in the air. I knew it was Azurine doing it. I didn't know how or what it meant, but I knew she was the cause behind the scent of rain permeating the cabin.

But it didn't matter.

She was my mate. Fated to join me in this life, practically made to be mine. Witch or wolf, human or not-so-much, she was mine. And I would honor that bond every day for as long as we were blessed to walk this earth together. Starting right now.

When I reached her, I put one hand on each side of her hips and loomed over her. She wasn't a short girl—not like Gates' mate, Kaija—but she was much smaller than I was. Delicate. Almost fragile when seen against me. And I wanted her against me. Wanted it in a way that made the rest of the world disappear. Wanted it with a single-minded focus that I had no power to fight.

Azurine didn't back away. Instead, she held my gaze, actually leaning into me as I surrounded her with my body. And when I had her where I wanted her, underneath me but without a single ounce of my weight resting on her, I touched my forehead to hers and sighed.

"I'm going to fall in with love you so hard. You'll never doubt my commitment to you."

Her breath raced from her mouth, a gusting exhale that I happily breathed in. She moved to grip my hand, her fingers hot and shaking, but perfect when tangled with my own. She brought her other hand to my face, soft against my skin as she lightly touched my cheek.

"I'm so scared of what this is," she whispered.

"This is us. Just you and me. The Fates brought us together, but we get to make all the rules." I touched my nose to hers, reveling in the contact. "We'll go as slow as you want, we'll get to know each other, and we'll take our time building a foundation. I make no demands of you other than to give me a chance. Let me show you how good it can be to be mated to a wolf. To be mine. My thread."

She shivered, her eyes never leaving mine. With more guts than I had, she leaned forward and pressed her lips to mine. Softly, a brush of a touch, but enough to set my world on end. The spirit of the wolf inside of me roared under the weight of his desires. I wanted her. In my bed and my arms. I wanted to cover her with my body and protect her from the world. I wanted to feed her, bathe her, and make her laugh. I wanted everything with her—I just had to convince her to want me, too.

Our kiss stayed chaste, sweet and closed-mouth. Eventually, she drew back, her eyes meeting mine and her tongue flashing as she licked her bottom lip. Her smile grew in time with mine, both of us breathless and flushed. With a glance down, she opened her mouth as if she were about to say something, but a loud bang outside made us both jerk. I jumped and spun, landing on the balls of my feet as I put myself between my mate and the door.

"Yo, Pup," Beast yelled from outside. "I think you and Glinda better get your asses out here."

"Glinda?" I whispered, practically to myself.

"The good witch from Oz. Your friend thinks he's got jokes." Azurine rose to her feet. I crowded her against the wall, needing her safe, fighting the urge to shift to my wolf form.

"It's okay," she said as she tried to push past me. "I can protect myself."

I growled and boxed her in until her back touched the wall, my body surrounding hers.

"Pup, calm down." She ran her hands over my head, through my hair, and down my back. Her touch was comforting, settling my wolf in a way words never would. She was safe. She was with me and she was safe.

I swallowed hard and closed my eyes, fighting to stop the rumble in my chest. "I'm trying."

Holding me close, she shushed me and kept her hands moving over my body. Eventually, I settled enough to reopen my eyes, meeting hers as my growl finally cut off.

"Sorry."

She shook her head. "Never apologize for your instincts or for wanting to protect me. I kind of like knowing I won't ever have to fight alone."

"Definitely not."

"Good." She smiled, her hands settling on my arms.

"You should wait inside. Let me go see what's happening out there."

Without warning, a green light lit up the window and a large boom shook the walls. Dust floated in the air as the cabin settled back onto its foundation. My wolf practically ripped himself from inside of me, forcing fur and claws to appear where skin and fingers had been seconds before. I growled and tried to push Azurine back against the wall, but she shook her head and grabbed my face, pinning me with her stare.

"I already know what's happening. My coven is here, and they're pissed, but they're also my family. Do not, under any circumstances, attack them." She brought her lips to my chin, kissing the gray fur that had appeared there. "Please."

I swallowed and nodded, not really sure if that was a promise I could keep.

SIX

"ANIMALS! RELEASE THE GIRL this instant."

I walked out of the cabin, letting Pup lead me. He was still struggling with his wolf, gray fur growing and receding with each breath. While I didn't mind the thought of his protectiveness, I knew he'd put himself in danger if he went up against my coven unprepared. There were some powerful witches in my group, and I had no doubts any one of them could take down a wolf shifter if they felt threatened.

Once Pup surveyed the area, he stepped out of my way, though still hovering and on guard. I walked to the edge of the porch, nearly rolling my eyes at the scene before me. Bethesda stood, hands up and long hair flowing, a bevy of gold bangle bracelets around her arms, appearing more carnival gypsy than witch born of the powerful Marrin line.

Scarlett leaned against the railing at the bottom of the steps with her arms crossed. She nodded her head when I looked her way. "I tried to tell her."

"What is she doing?" I asked.

"Saving you, apparently." Scarlett shrugged, and then tossed me my phone. "You dropped this."

Bethesda turned my way when Scarlett spoke, her scowl transforming to a surprised look. "Oh, thank the Goddess. Get over here, Weaver. I won't allow these animals to trick you into thinking you're some kind of chew toy."

Pup raised an eyebrow at me. "Chew toy?"

I shrugged. "Sure. Dogs like to chew on things."

"For the last time"—he leaned over me, a slight growl rumbling in his chest, his eyes so damn vibrant they almost glowed—"I'm not a dog. I'm a wolf."

I shivered, ignoring the calamity swirling around us as my coven and his friends stood in their tense showdown.

"I know." My voice came out breathy, much softer than normal. "You're a wolf, I'm your mate, and wolves mate for life."

"Exactly." He tangled his fingers with mine, pulling me close to him. "This is us; it's simple and small right now. A fated connection between two people. But this is going to be huge. We just have to give it time. Have to give us time."

I nodded, my fingertips positively tingling with how excited I was to spend more time with him. The talking and touching and kissing hadn't been enough. I wanted to drag him back in his cabin and curl up with him in his tiny bed. Wanted to wrap myself in his arms and have him tell me every story he knew. The thread between us was wrapped tight, holding me to him. I didn't want to stretch it any further than I absolutely had to. Screw my responsibilities. I had a soul mate who made me want to strip down and press my body against his.

Looming over me, leaning in for what I was sure was a kiss, Pup licked his bottom lip. My eyes tracked the motion, wanting to feel that wet heat on various parts of my body. But those delicious thoughts were interrupted by the shrill yell of Bethesda.

"Weaver, get your ass over here right now."

I blinked, shaking off the lust and disappointment swamping me. Shrugging, I gave Pup a small smile. "My ass has been beckoned."

"It's a phenomenal ass. It really should be invited more places. Like say, my cabin…later tonight." He gave me what can only be described as a wolfish grin as I laughed.

"Nice try, Romeo. But I think the only place my ass is going to be is my bed."

"Can't blame a guy for trying."

I laughed, shaking my head at his boyishness. Knowing I needed to say goodbye, I stepped into the warmth of his body. I wanted to hug him; I wanted to wrap my arms around his neck and squeeze him.

And I really didn't want to leave.

But my covenmates were capable of all sorts of craziness if they thought they were in danger. I had to go so I could find a way to explain things to them. They needed to accept that these men, these wolf shifters, were not witch hunters. They were not a danger to us, especially not my Pup.

Before I could leave him, though, I needed to know he would be safe. I had an urge to offer him protection, from what, I had no idea, but there was no denying the instinct. Listening to the guidance being offered, I leaned into his hold, pursing my lips and blowing against his throat.

"What are you doing?" he asked, quiet but unafraid.

Once I'd finished, I gave him a small, sarcastic glare. "Just hush and trust me."

I took a step back, but his hand caught my elbow and held me in place. His eyes burned into mine, strong and true as he whispered a single word that nearly brought me to my knees.

"Always."

I sighed and brushed my fingers over his lips. "Sweet boy."

He leaned over me, placing his forehead against mine. "Do

your worst."

Smirking, I shook my head at his sass. But with witches and shifters arguing in the background, I knew my time was limited. There were many protection spells I could have cast, calling on any number of Goddesses and Gods to infuse me with their power. But my Pup was strong; he was able to defend himself if needed. I chose a simple spell taught to all witches early in their training, one requiring no cast circle or magickal elements to improve the spell's potency. No, I chose a spell that would rely solely on my connection to the protected and the faith I put in my own power.

So with my Pup strong in my mind, I closed my eyes and concentrated on my bond to the earth, the wind, the water, and the fire that made up the world around me. Stepping slowly, never breaking contact with him, I circled Pup, chanting as I went.

"Thrice round the circle's bound, sink all evil to the ground. Take my words and listen thee, guard him from thine enemy." Three times I walked around him, repeating the words over and over again. When I returned to my starting point after the third circle, I stopped and opened my eyes, meeting his stare. "So mote it be."

He had such a handsome smile on his face, slightly confused but totally accepting. It stunned me—how open he was to all the things being with me entailed. He didn't question or judge, didn't try to get me to explain every word and movement. He let me be me, and that was something I appreciated.

Unable to resist, I reached for him. Pup reciprocated the motion immediately, bringing his hand to meet mine. Our fingers touched, entwining softly even as I took a step backward.

"Merry meet, Pup of the Feral Breed."

His eyes burned with his inner fire. Our arms rose, fingers straining to stay together as the distance between us grew.

When we finally broke contact, he swallowed hard, looking completely broken as he watched me go.

"Will you be back?"

"Soon." I walked backward toward my coven, still not wanting to leave him. "I'll come see you very soon."

He nodded once as the other men in the group joined him on the porch. They made an impressive wall—all handsome and muscled. And while Pup was the biggest of the three, the other two looked deadly in a way Pup's baby face would never allow.

"You'll keep your paws far away from our coven," Bethesda yelled from behind me. "You may claim you're not witch hunters, but that doesn't mean we want your kind around our young ones. Come near the Weavers again, and I'll release the full power of this coven against you."

Bethesda grabbed my arm and pulled me away from the cabin, making me stumble. I heard Pup's growl, but he stood in shadows on the porch, making it impossible to see his face. Not that I needed to. He would be fierce in his anger at my being handled so roughly, of that I was certain.

Once I had my footing, I turned to follow Bethesda to the group of women surrounding the trailhead that would lead us to the lighthouse. Sarah stood at the rear of the group, looking pale and small with Amber by her side.

"You should have called me right away," Bethesda growled in my ear, distracting me from Sarah and Amber. "If we'd known there were witch hunters in this camp, we would have come for you sooner."

"They're not witch hunters."

"They live in concert with the wolf; they cannot be trusted."

I huffed and pulled my arm from her grasp. Before she could grab me again, I turned toward the wall of men, meeting the eyes of Charlotte, who stood on the steps with them.

"Help me out here. They're not witch hunters, are they?"

Charlotte shrugged. "Not that I know of, though I'm still pretty new here. Rebel, do you hunt witches?"

The blond man shook his head. "No. Traditionally the witch hunters are full Weres, not shifters. I believe they call themselves the 'Hounds of God.'"

Charlotte nodded. "See? Not witch hunters. Wait…what do you mean full Weres?"

"Werewolves." Rebel shrugged, as if admitting werewolves truly walked the earth was not a big deal. And maybe it wasn't to a man who went from human to wolf in the blink of an eye.

"Well, that's…terrifying." Charlotte shivered and looked my way. "Things just keep getting weirder around here."

I shrugged and faced Bethesda. "See? Not witch hunters."

"Their concubine can deny the evil within them all she wants, but we can sense the hunter in them. They are a danger to all of us." Bethesda raised her arms as if to perform a spell, but I grabbed them and pushed them down as a vicious growl filled the night around us.

"They're not hunters. The pull I felt brought me here for a reason, and I won't allow you to hurt them when they've done nothing wrong." I looked deep into her eyes, making sure she understood my point. "Free will of all and harm of none."

She glared at me. "Have you lost your mind? They're hunters, even if they choose to lie about it. I'm protecting my coven."

I shook my head. "No. I'm that man's mate, and I won't have you hurt him."

She looked shocked, her expression one of surprise and rage. "You cannot mean to breed with a dog?"

"He's not a dog." I looked over at Pup, who'd moved into the firelight at the bottom of the steps. "He's not a hunter, but he is a wolf. I'm his mate and he's my…" I shrugged, unwilling to share the part of him being my thread. That information was for him and me alone; I didn't want anyone ruining the moment with their disbelief. Pup gave me a smile, though his was small and forced.

"Oh, for the love of the Goddess." Bethesda grabbed my arm and turned to the rest of the group of witches waiting for her direction. "They've brainwashed the middle one. Let's go back to the lighthouse so we can talk some sense into these girls."

She pushed me forward as the rest of our group began creeping into the darkened woods. Feeling the thread between Pup and me grow tight and painful, I took one more look at the men of the Feral Breed. Pup stood at the head of them, stepping closer as I watched. He looked as upset by our parting as I felt. I wished I could run back to him and find comfort in his arms.

"I tried to tell them." Scarlett came to stand beside me, looking bored and tired. "Do they not realize I would've burned this place to the ground if I thought they were hunters? Please."

Bethesda looked at each of us in turn then glared at the wolves. "We'll deal with this so-called mating business when we get home. Do not attempt to follow us, beasts."

"Yes, ma'am. We'll wait to hear from you." Rebel yelled from behind us. I turned again, peeking at him over my shoulder. Rebel glanced at Pup before meeting my gaze, his eyes practically glowing and his face serious. "Come back soon, Azurine. It's not pleasant for a wolf to be separated from their mate."

I nodded, my eyes going to Pup. "Soon. I promise."

The third man, Beast, stepped forward as we reached the trailhead. "Your time is nearing its end."

Witches gasped and spun, moving into defensive stances. Beast's words sounded like a threat, like the coven was in danger. My blood ran cold as I waited for some sort of attack, though nothing came. Beast stood calmly, tall and stoic, neither threatening further nor apologizing for his words. My eyes flitted to Pup, who was watching me, worry etched on his handsome face.

"Is that some kind of threat?" Scarlett asked as she let the fire within dance on the ends of her fingers.

Beast rolled his eyes. "Easy there, burner. I've got no plans to raid your henhouse." He pointed at Sarah. "I can smell your death approaching. Do you have access to medical care?"

Bethesda stepped in front of Sarah. "We take care of our own, hunter."

Beast huffed. "Well, that's all fine and dandy, but she's got something rotten inside of her. Chamomile tea and mint leaves may not be enough."

Sarah sighed, looking even more exhausted than she had seconds before. Cautiously, she stepped from behind Bethesda and gave the men a small smile.

"Thank you for your concern, but I trust my coven to take care of me."

Beast nodded reluctantly. Sarah, Amber, and Bethesda walked into the woods, leaving Scarlett and me alone at the edge of the forest. My sister met my gaze, looking just as concerned as I felt. Sarah had been our rock, our guardian, since we'd been left with the coven. And while we all knew she was sick, I don't think any of us was ready to hear that her time to leave us for the Summerlands was drawing close.

Without words, Scarlett hurried into the tree line, following the rest of the coven. I trailed after her, my heart practically tearing in two. On one side, it wanted to follow Sarah, the woman who'd raised my sisters and me. To comfort her and spend as much time with her as possible before her end. On the other, it wanted to stay at the camp with Pup. To explore our connection and find comfort in his arms.

"Weaver!" Bethesda's shrill yell cut through the confusion in my mind, and my body followed her call as it had so many times in the past.

"Bye, Azurine," Charlotte called. "Come see us soon."

I waved, wondering when the last time was someone in my coven had used my real name. Sarah and my sisters did, of course. But the rest of the women tended to call us by our surname. We were the Weavers, the orphaned triplets left with their leader. And though I'd always considered them my family, the simple use of my first name by a woman I'd just met had made me suddenly wonder if I was missing something.

SEVEN

Azurine

THE WALK TO THE lighthouse was filled with a wary anxiety every one of us had to feel. Scarlett stayed close to my side while Amber and Sarah walked just ahead of us. None of us spoke through the woods and across the sand on the way to the only home I'd ever known. And yet it wasn't where I wanted to be. At all.

"Weavers," Bethesda said as we entered through the front door. "Go wait in the hall. The coven needs to be updated. Sarah, I want you resting."

I watched as Sarah nodded, exhaustion plain to see on her face. She gave us each a small, dry kiss on the cheek before heading for the stairs. Amber, Scarlett, and I followed Bethesda down the foyer and through the kitchen to the back hallway. A low bench sat on one wall across from a set of double doors. The doors led to the coven's meeting room, the storage area for magick supplies, a library of documents and teaching books, and the fireproof safe where the grimoire rested.

The centuries-old book explained the origin of the Parity Lake coven, how our magick manifested, and the spells our ancestors had built. It also had tips on everything from growing nettles in the winter to identifying hunters and other beings outside the norm. As I sat on the bench and my mind drifted to Pup, I wondered if there was a section on shifters and anything about their mating bonds. Maybe the coven would be willing to accept my relationship with Pup if I could find something in the grimoire about shifters versus werewolves.

"I can't believe you did this, Zuri." Amber paced the length of the hall, shaking her head and looking altogether angry. "You knew there could be hunters in the area, yet you did nothing when you found a pack of them in the woods. How are we supposed to defend ourselves with you fraternizing with the enemy?"

"They're not hunters." Scarlett slouched against the wall, sounding bored.

"And what"—Amber threw her hands up—"now you're the all-knowing expert on witch hunters? You think just because they say they're not hunters that they're telling the truth? You're just as stupid as she is."

"Hey." I jumped to my feet, tired and confused and wishing I was back in the dirty little cabin with the man with no last name. That wouldn't stop me from defending myself, though. "You don't get to insult either of us. Something led me to that camp and to Pup. I'm his fated mate, and I trust him when he says they're not hunters."

"Right." Amber snorted and shook her head. "I mean, he and his friends just happen to be staying at the edge of our property, showing up right around the time we start seeing a witch hunter, but he's not a witch hunter. And he turns into a giant wolf, just like a wolf hunter, but he's not a witch hunter. And now, you're telling me I should believe that you're some kind of soul mate of his, that the two of you were joined together by the Fates as you waited to be reincarnated in the Summerlands. Sure, that makes sense."

"You don't know," I exclaimed, my face burning. This was why I hadn't told them. Why I refused to say he was my red thread. The mocking and disbelief Amber was showing was a perfect example of my need to keep this secret. "You have no idea what happened. You weren't there."

Amber spun and came at me, stopping when she was mere inches away. "You're right. I wasn't there. None of us were because when we were coming together to protect our coven, *our family*, you chose to run off and play the dating game with your dog."

"Quit being a bitch." Scarlett glared at our sister from where she leaned against the wall. "Sarah told us to follow Zuri's pull. It's not as if we just decided to go for a stroll through the woods for no reason."

"Nice," Amber spat. "I challenge Zuri on her choices and I'm the bitch? How about she's the bitch for running off and putting this stupid pull she keeps complaining about ahead of her coven. How about you're a bitch for following her and not notifying the coven of the danger the two of you had put us all in. How about both of you are bitches for abandoning your family and friends when we needed your help."

"What are you talking about?" I asked. "Sarah *told* us to go."

Amber shook her head, her eyes growing red and wet. "The Marrins will explain."

"You're our sister." I reached for her, but she pulled away, glaring at my proffered hand. "Why do we have to wait for the Marrins to tell us anything?"

Amber spun. "Because you chose a man over your family."

"That's enough, Weavers." Bethesda stood in the open doorway to the coven room, surprising all of us. "Come inside, girls. There's much to discuss."

Amber huffed and hurried past Bethesda as Scarlett raised

her eyebrows at me. I shrugged and walked into the room, every nerve I had feeling frayed and trampled.

The three leaders of the coven families sat at a curved table on the far side of the room, one representative each from the Marrins, the Bishops, and the Gardners. For the first time, something about the setup struck me as incomplete. Sarah had raised us, therefore we'd always been somewhat included in the Bishop family. But technically, we were our own family. As part of the coven, we should have had someone sitting at that table, someone representing the Weavers. Amber should have been seated at that table instead of hovering to the side.

Clara Gardner walked around the perimeter of the room, chanting and pointing her knifelike athame in a manner that spoke of protection. The ceremonial dagger glinted in the candlelight, the double-edged blade slicing through the air with every sweep of Clara's arm. Though similar to the spell I cast for Pup before leaving camp, this one focused on protecting our secrets and our fellow coven members from dark energies.

A single white candle burned on the altar, one that was never snuffed. In a home ruled by magick, no candles were lit without thought to color and meaning. White enhanced our link to the pure spirits and to the elemental magick within. It was a cleansing color, one of purification and truth-seeking. But around the perimeter of the room, darker candles burned. And they made my blood boil.

"What's going on here?" I asked.

Amber's eyes darted around the room, an almost guilty expression on her face. Black candles rested upon every flat surface. From tables to bookshelves, window ledges to open space on the floor. Their placement and selection could not have been accidental. The color black was one of protection and safety. Of counteracting negative energies and repelling dark magick. Of reversing curses.

Bethesda glared from the Marrin family seat at the leaders' table. "You will not disrespect this gathering by refusing to follow the rules."

"Ladies, please." Siobhan, Sarah's niece, took a seat behind the table, looking sad and tired. "Let's not get bogged down in red tape and ridiculous fanfare no one cares about. We have grave little time for planning."

Clara huffed but continued on her way, pointing the athame in the corners and calling upon the guardians to watch over us. No one spoke as Clara finished her casting, addressing the room in full.

"Let all those who choose to remain in this sacred and protected space do so in perfect love and perfect trust." She dropped three iron nails into a pot of earth near the doors, pushing the metal deep in the soil. Ensuring our protection from dark energies. Once finished, she shuffled to the table and took her seat to the right of Siobhan, the place for the head of the Gardner family.

"We found paw prints around the back porch. Huge prints that are too large to be a coyote or domestic dog. My aunt…" Siobhan swallowed, looking to Bethesda as if for support.

"We believe a hunter is responsible. The stink of the hunter was all over the porch and by the kitchen windows. He was watching us this evening." Bethesda's voice was grave, her words clipped. "It's time for us to leave, but Sarah refuses. She intends to die here."

The room began to spin as the words sank in. I reached for Scarlett at the same time she reached for me, both of us staring at a teary Siobhan, who watched us with red-rimmed eyes.

"We've consulted the grimoire," Clara added. "There's nothing that can be done to stop the progression of the cancer plaguing her lungs."

"No, you're wrong," Scarlett spat. "There must be

something. We're witches, for fuck's sake. We should be able to heal a little cancer."

"You will respect the coven and watch your language, Weaver." Clara sat, athame in hand, glaring at Scarlett.

"Fuck the coven. We need answers; there has to be something in those moldy old books that can help her."

As the handful of witches in the room huffed and hollered in response to Scarlett's disrespect, Siobhan turned my way. The tears that rolled down her face matched mine.

"How long?"

Siobhan sniffed and dropped her gaze to the tabletop. "A few weeks at most."

"And there are no spells or potions we can brew?" I asked. "Nothing we can do to help her?"

She shook her head. "No, dear. Amber and I spent a few hours in the kitchen brewing a tincture that will keep her comfortable as her time ends, but that's all she wants. That and to die in the house in which she's lived her entire life."

"There has to be something," Scarlett said, her voice rough and angry.

"There was something." Amber appeared behind Siobhan, her face filled with rage. "There were healing and longevity spells we could have tried. But the coven is already breaking apart. Witches are running and hiding, leaving a handful of us to deal with the work. And you…you were off cavorting with the enemy. Was that him watching Siobhan and me through the window? Or was it one of his friends?"

"Amber Jane." Scarlett turned a heated glare on our sister, but to no avail. The woman was staring at me with a scowl on her face.

"They're not hunters; they're shapeshifters. And the Fates…"

I trailed off, suddenly afraid to share the information of my bond to Pup. The coven knew he saw me as his mate, but I was holding back the part about him being my red thread. The room no longer felt safe, the comfort I'd long expected in the space where I'd first learned string and color magick gone.

"Because what?" Bethesda asked. "They wanted to see if the secrets of the Weaver triplets were true? That you're as easy to bang as a broken screen door?"

"That's enough." Siobhan went to stand, but Amber put a hand on her shoulder to keep her in her seat.

"No," Amber said. "I know Sarah told them to run toward Zuri's pull, but they should have come home as soon as they realized they were wolves in men's bodies. Werewolf or shapeshifter, they're all the same. Evil, out-of-control animals who want nothing more than to decimate covens like ours."

A fog began to roll in across the floor as the rage I felt heated me from the inside out. "They're not evil."

Amber glanced at the fog and smirked. With a flick of her fingers, she created a draft that made the fog clear the room once more. Bethesda smiled from her place beside her before giving me a look that spoke of nothing but disgust and disdain.

"They're animals, mindless killers of our kind. But you let them manipulate you, didn't you?" Bethesda leaned over the table, resting her weight on her hands. "I saw you kiss that dog. Did you lay with him, too? Were you going to breed with that animal and make some kind of perverted witch-wolf babies?"

"You bitch." I jumped at the table, but Scarlett grabbed me and held me back, her fingers burning me through my clothes.

"That's enough!" Bethesda moved out from behind the table, a dark energy wrapped around her like a cloak. "Let's get this over with now. Azurine Eugenia Weaver, you've betrayed your coven and disrespected the family who took you in when you were left on our doorstep. You've brought death and chaos to this coven with the thoughtlessness of your actions. I hereby ask the coven to initiate a shunning."

My heart stuttered. Shunned? For following the pull of the Fates leading me to the man who held the end of my red thread? It was impossible, incomprehensible. A shunning would make me an outsider in my own coven—able to live with the witches and participate in any necessary chores, but otherwise ignored. Unable to attend magickal gatherings. Unable to research through the library or participate in training exercises. Witches were shunned for breaking the covenants of the coven or dabbling in magicks tinged with negative energy. I'd done neither.

Bethesda looked around the room at the witches scattered about. "Who here supports my call for shunning? Let the coven speak."

As the first witch raised her hand—a woman who'd painted my nails as a child and taught me how to swirl my hot cocoa with magick instead of a spoon—my stomach fell and my heart seized in my chest.

"Wait."

The witches ignored my plea, more of them raising their hands in support of a punishment our coven hadn't issued in a hundred years. But the worst moment, the one that practically ripped the heart out of my chest and stomped on it, was when Amber slowly raised her hand. She stared at me as that pale hand went above her shoulder, anger on her face and burning in her eyes. She could have stabbed me with an athame and not shocked me more.

"The majority have spoken," Bethesda said, glaring at Siobhan, who had not raised her hand against me. "Consider yourself shunned, Azurine Weaver."

Clara stood from her place and shuffled toward the doors. "The circle is open yet unbroken." She kissed her athame before thrusting it into the same dirt-filled vase in which she'd buried the iron nails. The soil grounded the powers into the earth, releasing the deities and showing respect to the elements we relied upon. It was a ritual I'd watched and participated in since I was a small child, one I knew by heart. And knowing it could be the last time I saw it performed in this room made my soul scream.

When the witches had left, Amber included, Scarlett and I stood in front of Siobhan, all of us looking shell-shocked.

"What did you do?" Siobhan whispered. I gasped as tears once again fell from my eyes, the blame she laid at my feet hurting more than the actual shunning. She came around the table and wrapped her arms around me, holding me close. "You must fix this, Zuri. I can't go against the coven. Once my mom's gone, there will be no one to fight for you. Prove yourself now while she can stand behind you."

"I…" I choked on a sob as the thought of losing my family battled with the thought of never seeing Pup again. I'd only just met him, but I knew. I *knew* he was meant to be mine. He was important in my life, my red thread, the man made for me by the Fates. And though no witch currently a part of the Parity Coven had ever formed an attachment to a man for longer than the time it took to become pregnant, I knew my bond to Pup was something unbreakable. The Fates led me to him. They would never steer me wrong.

"Hush now." Siobhan stroked my hair and gave me a dry-lipped kiss on my cheek. "Off to bed with you. When morning comes, we'll cast a net of protection around the house for Mom since she refuses to leave. Amber's already said she'll stay with her until the hunter is destroyed. I wish I could stay, but I'm taking all the witchlings up to Munising to hide. Stay strong, but don't go back into the woods. We'll get through this hunter mess, and then we can all work together to help you end this manipulative curse."

I stepped back, my blood like ice as her words settled in my head. She didn't believe me. None of my coven did, not even my older sister. Only Scarlett was on my side.

"I need to get a few things in order, girls." Siobhan let me go with a sigh, not realizing how much she'd just broken my heart. "Head on up to bed. We'll meet in the greenhouse first thing in the morning."

I turned for the doors, my body and mind numb with grief. Scarlett led me out of the room, neither of us speaking. The night had taken a horrible turn. From Amber's betrayal to the loss of almost my entire support system, everything coven-related had crashed in a sea of negative energy and fetid air.

"This is crazy," Scarlett said as we reached the stairs. "All the bullshit the witches in this coven have pulled, and yet you're the one shunned. And for what? So your soul mate gets a little fuzzy now and again. At least he doesn't pee on the floor." Her eyes opened wide and her mouth fell open as she looked at me. "Oh, please tell me he doesn't pee on the floor. That would just be too much to handle, even for me."

I shook my head as we climbed to the top of the stairs, thankful in ways I'd never thought possible for my relationship with Scarlett. "I didn't see any sign of urination when I was in the cabin," I deadpanned.

"Well, thank fuck for that." Scarlett headed to her bedroom door, pausing with her hand on the knob. "We'll figure something out, Zuri. No one's going to break up our family, not even our own sister."

I nodded, my eyes burning. I watched as Scarlett disappeared into her room before walking into my own. And though I'd grown up in the same room, lived in it since they stopped letting Amber, Scarlett, and me sleep in a crib together, it felt altogether wrong. White walls, whitewashed floorboards, white furniture. The entire room looked as if a snowman had thrown up in it, though the intention had been to keep the energies close and pure. It was why the entire interior of the lighthouse was white. Every inch devoid of color unless needed for a particular purpose.

I'd never really thought about my space in the lighthouse before. But right then, it was absolutely the last place I wanted to be. Too pale, too bright, too…not me. I longed for warm, dark floors, for dark plywood walls and simple furnishings, for a cabin where a man slept in a quilt-covered bed. Or perhaps he didn't sleep. Perhaps he was awake, sitting around a fire in the cool night air. Perhaps he was reading a book or staring at the ceiling. And maybe, just maybe, he was thinking of me.

I slid down the closed door and brought my knees to my chest. Focusing on reaching a place of peace and enlightenment, I slowed my breathing. The pain in my heart receded as I focused on nothing more than my next inhalation. Time rolled past without witness, allowing me my moment of calm and reflection. I opened myself to the love and guidance of the Goddess, to the energy of the element of air, Amber's favored element. And while I had a stronger grip on water magick, air was the element of vision and voice. I needed to think, to pick my path. Needed to decide whether it was right to stay with my coven and fight for their acceptance or…something else. I needed to see a way to be rid of the hunter no matter my choice. So I breathed, and I called the air to me. And I was quiet.

The inky darkness of my mind slowly opened, revealing lights and pictures from years past. Memories I'd not thought of for over a decade trickled in, bringing me back to my witchling years. The time before my powers truly developed, when I wanted to immerse myself in magick every day and my biggest dream was to master the elemental earth power like Sarah. My memories played through a random summer day, one when I'd snuck into the ritual room to spend time alone reading the coven grimoire. I'd done it often, sometimes dragging Scarlett and Amber with me.

But this memory played out with me alone, the heavy, leather-bound book resting in my lap as I read the spells, the rituals, the hand-written notes from witches recent and centuries past. I'd spend hours carefully flipping pages and devouring information. Yet in my memory, I wasn't turning a page. I wasn't mouthing words or chanting under my breath. I sat, stunned and still, my eyes scanning one particular page over and over again.

"Oh, Zuri." Sarah strolled into the remembered ritual room, and my younger self looked up at her with something like confusion on her face. "One of these days someone else is going to catch you and you're really going to be in trouble."

"You'd never let me get into too much trouble."

Sarah laughed, coming to sit beside me. "Very true. There'll never come a day that I won't be there to save you or your sisters. I promise." She pushed my dark hair behind my ear and gave me a watery smile. "You look so much like your mother."

"Her name is under these notes." I held the book out to her. "Is that her handwriting?"

Sarah seemed surprised by the question before focusing on the grimoire. "Yes, that's her script. She always had much neater penmanship than I did."

Younger me traced the cursive words with a single finger, brow furrowed. "I've never seen her writing before. It looks a lot like mine."

Sarah smiled and pulled the book into her own lap. "Yes, it certainly does. We've all written notes and comments over the years, especially your mom. She had an obsession with researching obscure information and leaving notes in this book. Let's see if we can find more from your mom."

As the two sat closer so they could share the grimoire, the

memory faded and I returned to the present. My cheeks burned from the tears streaming down my face, and my breathing was harsh. She was dying. The woman who'd stepped in without complaint when our mother died in childbirth, clinging to Sarah's hand and begging her to take care of us. And she did; Sarah had raised us as her own. She'd fought for us and protected us for over two decades.

For minutes that lasted long past the point of comfort, I sobbed, quieting the sounds with my knees pressed to my face. We had so little family; losing Sarah would be a huge blow to my sisters and me. Coven be damned, their loss of a friend and mentor would never compare to what the three of us were about to have ripped away.

Without warning, a single solitary wolf howl sounded, breaking the silence of the night. A tingle raced down my spine as the lonely sound ripped through the air, a feeling of rightness and purpose. The thread tying me to Pup drew taut around my heart. Pulling me. Leading me once more. And I refused to deny it.

I stood on shaky legs and walked toward the single window, moving faster with each step. Throwing open the sash and screen, I hurried to crawl over the sill. My feet slipped on the tin of the overhang below, but I held on to the edge and caught my balance before letting go. Before rushing to escape.

I shuffled down the incline, careful and quiet. When I reached the edge of the little roof over the back porch, I hopped down and rolled through my landing. Relief washed over me as I felt the grass beneath me. Jumping to my feet, I looked over my shoulder. The house was dark, quiet in a way that spoke of death and not just sleep. The darkness made me shiver hard, the cold air not helping at all.

Within seconds, I was running south. Through trees, over sand, along the lake—my pace stayed steady and my feet flew.

The dark and cold didn't matter. I needed Pup, the handsome man with the missing surname. I needed the warmth his presence gave me. Needed the quiet comfort I'd found with him.

Everything within my soul told me I needed to be with him.

The camp was dark and quiet as I hurried through the tree line. And while I wondered briefly if I was intruding or trespassing where I didn't belong, I also felt a sense of relief just knowing Pup and I were on the same property. And yet, I doubted. I stood and argued with myself over the best way to let him know I was there until a voice shattered the darkness.

"He's sleeping, but I know he'd love to see you."

Charlotte sat on the step leading to a cabin next to the one Pup was staying in. She wore a ridiculously large sweatshirt and pajama pants with what looked like dancing penguins printed on them. With her hair up in a ponytail and no makeup, she looked about sixteen.

"I'm sorry. I wasn't going to bother—"

She waved me off. "Sure you were, but you faltered there at the end."

I nodded. "I'm a little…confused tonight."

She leaned back on her hands and looked up at the sky. "I know that feeling. Like falling for them would be the absolute worst and best thing ever. Like being with them would be the hardest and best choice in your life." She looked over at me once more. "Like your entire future is right through that door, but if you open it, you have to lose everything you've ever known and loved."

I crept closer, desperate to see Pup and yet intrigued by her view of my situation. "Like I'd have to give up my life to be a part of his and wondering how I could be so certain it would be worth it."

She nodded. "Like you'll have to mourn the loss of your family and friends being in your life while celebrating the amount of love you have for him."

"I refuse to mourn for my sisters."

"As I refuse to mourn for my brother, the only family I have left, and yet here we are." She stood, pushing her blond hair back as the wind caught it. "My name's Charlotte Andrews. I found out I was the mate to a wolf shifter just seven months ago, so I'm no expert. But if you ever need an ear, you can use mine."

"Thanks. I appreciate that. And I'm Azurine Weaver, but everyone calls me Zuri."

"Well, Zuri, I can guess that there are two men wide awake right now. One of the downsides to this whole extravaganza is the heightened senses these boys have. You lose your privacy and your ability to have a secret." She glanced over her shoulder at the door to the cabin and sighed. "They're probably getting a little cranky, waiting for us to join them."

I looked over to the cabin where Pup was staying, butterflies taking flight in my stomach.

"What if he doesn't want me here?"

Before she could answer, the door to Pup's cabin opened and the man himself stepped onto the porch in nothing but a pair of tight-fitting boxers. The light of the nearly full moon highlighted the dips and curves of his muscles, the shadows deepening every ridge. He looked like a living statue, some long-dead warrior brought back to life and placed on that porch just for me.

Charlotte chuckled. "Somehow I think your question's already been answered." She grabbed my hand and gave me a smile. "I know how you feel, Zuri."

"How do I know what to do?" My question was soft, quiet, yet Pup cocked his head as if he'd heard me. And maybe he had, though I doubted he'd be the one to help me find the answer.

Charlotte's smile fell as the door to her cabin opened behind her, Rebel leaning his shoulder against the doorframe.

"I'm still trying to figure that out." Charlotte pasted on a happy face and turned. The man in the doorway looked her over, inspecting her, before frowning and taking a step back into the darkness of the cabin. Charlotte followed him, shutting the door behind her with a quiet snick. Long after they'd disappeared, I stood, staring at Pup, frozen on the grass. He didn't move toward me, didn't try to tempt me or cajole me into joining him. He stood and waited, giving me the time to work through my thoughts. And when I did, when I knew that, for at least one night, he was worth the risk I was taking, I straightened my shoulders and took a single step in his direction. That one move brought a smile to his face, and my heart melted at the sight. No longer willing to wait, I rushed to him, reaching for his hand before I even made it to the steps.

"Hi." I smiled as he pulled me into his arms. He was so warm, so hard and yet gentle at the same time.

"Hi." His voice was deep and smooth, sending shivers up my spine. "It's late. Why don't you come to bed?"

I stepped back, out of his arms. The cold of the night air settled around me, making me curl in on myself as my doubts raged inside my head. "I'm not—"

"Not that." He smiled and tugged me closer. Never pulling or demanding, he guided me inside the warm little cabin and shut the door behind him. With his hands on my hips, he directed me to the bed in the corner. "I'll sleep on the floor if you like, but if you're willing to share a bed with me, I promise to be a perfect gentleman. I just want you to lay with me."

Perfect…he was perfect in that moment, giving me exactly what I needed and taking nothing in return. I nodded as he sat on the mattress and slid over to give me room. Craving comfort,

I pulled my sweatshirt over my head, leaving me in nothing but a thin tank top. Before I could think twice, I unbuttoned my jeans and tugged them down my legs, kicking them off. Pup watched me, his eyes bright but not aggressive. He didn't make me feel on display or uncomfortable. Instead, his watchfulness made me feel warm and safe. At home.

I knelt on the edge of the mattress and shuffled forward before lying down beside him. The bed was small, but there was plenty of room for the two of us as we cuddled in the center.

Pup dragged the blanket over us, tucking it in behind my shoulders. Once covered, he pulled me tight against his chest and wrapped me in his arms. The warmth, the feeling of comfort, the contact he gave me was better than any sleeping tincture the coven could brew. My eyelids drooped as Pup sighed into my hair and held me close.

"I'm so glad you came back."

"Me too." I yawned and squirmed in his grasp. Finally, my head found the perfect niche between Pup's bicep and his shoulder. I snuggled into his hold, breathing in his earthy scent and allowing the late hour to settle over me

And then I surrendered to sleep.

EIGHT

Pup

I WOKE WITH A start, clinging to the woman who'd literally fallen into my life and taken ownership of my heart. She lay sleeping in my arms, her head on my bicep. Peaceful. Unlike when she'd shown up in camp the night before. Then she'd been a mess of tangled emotions, a woman in distress. I didn't know what had upset her to the point that she'd left her home in the middle of the night to come find me, but I was glad she had. Having her here with me was exactly what I wanted.

I yawned and pressed my nose into Zuri's hair so I could breathe her in. Find a moment of peace with her. I'd been on edge the night before, knowing she was out of my grasp. I wanted to shift and follow her scent through the woods to her home, but Rebel and Beast kept me busy with information on the den in Kalamazoo. I'd need to head down there later today, but for the moment, I was happily wrapped around my mate, and I fully intended on staying in this spot for as long as possible.

The K-zoo theft was the best-timed job I'd ever had because it had allowed me to find my mate. It was also the worst-timed job for the same reason. Though I was newly mated and completely out of my mind with the protective instincts that came with the presence of Azurine in my life, Rebel was expecting results. I needed figure out where the hell this Spook guy was and drag his sorry ass back to the camp for retribution. It would take me a day at most, maybe less if I got lucky on information. That wasn't too bad.

But my heart lurched at the thought of leaving Zuri for that long. It was hard enough when she walked into the woods with those other witches. Then she'd been with her family, with others like her who would help to keep her safe. I knew I had to let her leave with them. Driving out of camp without her on the back of my bike was going to hurt like a bitch. I didn't want to leave her behind. I hated the thought of not being here if she needed me again. But I couldn't fail Rebel, not this time. So I curled around Zuri in the darkness and held her close while I could, breathing in her scent and basking in her warmth.

As the hours went from the darkness of predawn to the peachy glow of early morning, Azurine began to show signs of wakefulness. Her temperature rose, her breathing quickened, and her heart picked up its pace. After a few moments, her arms tightened their hold on me and her leg came up to wrap around my hip. All the way up around my hip. My erection practically cried at the unfairness of being so close to exactly where it wanted to go but unable to dive in. I did my best to think of things that would make him stand down, but he refused. Our mate was near, and he wanted to get at her.

Ignoring how badly I wanted to fuck her through the mattress, I kissed the top of her head and curled around her even more. If someone walked in, they probably wouldn't even be able to see Zuri, what with the way I hovered over her. But I liked it, and my wolf liked it—our mate was safe and warm. That was all that mattered.

As I watched her peaceful face, she blinked her eyes open.

At first she appeared confused, and her body stiffened in my arms. I was about to let her go when she finally lifted her eyes to meet mine.

"Hi," she whispered as her body relaxed once again in my hold. Her voice practically made me whimper. I had such a need for her, a deep and endless craving. I could hardly hold myself back from my need to devour her. My dick was painfully hard after being pressed up against her soft girl-flesh all night, not to mention the way her position made him brush against the cotton panties covering her. Part of me wanted to tilt my hips away so she wouldn't know how she made me lust after her. But the rest of me…

"Good morning." I rolled us, ending with her upon my chest and straddling my hips. My dick resting between us. I didn't move, just let her lay on me, her own weight pressing those soft curves against the part of me that was obviously happy to see her.

With a sigh, she ran her hands over my pecs and down my arms. Once her fingers hit my elbows, she reversed her path, lighting me on fire from within with nothing more than a few strokes of her hands. I flattened my hands against her back and did the same, sliding them up and down her soft skin, relishing all the skin-to-skin contact.

I moaned and closed my eyes when she scraped her nails over my nipple. She chuckled and did it again before leaning over to place a single soft kiss to the center of my chest.

I pushed her hair back over her shoulders and smiled. "Did you sleep okay?"

"Better than ever." She sighed and laid her head on my shoulder, her hair tickling me suddenly the most erotic thing I'd ever experienced. I held back a growl even as my hips flexed of their own accord. She rode the movement, her own body arching into me.

But then she groaned.

"I have to go home."

I growled and whimpered, unable to hold it back. I didn't want her to leave. I wanted her to stay with me. I wanted her to keep rubbing me, to lay with me, to let me run my hands over her body. I wanted every moment to be with her, but deep down, I knew I needed to follow her lead. If Rebel and Charlotte had taught me anything, it was that the woman needed time to accept the relationship. The depth of the mating bond wasn't something they could relate to. This was no "Hi, I love you. Let's get married" thing; it was more of a "Hi, you're mine. Don't ever leave my sight" thing.

Which sounded supercreepy when I thought of it like that.

I didn't want Zuri to feel trapped or suffocated; I just wanted her with me. But she had a life elsewhere, one with family and friends she cared about. I couldn't steal her away from all that. I sort of envied Gates his finding a mate in a shewolf—at least Kaija understood how a mating worked and accepted him from the start. Zuri may not have been human, but she sure as hell wasn't a shifter, either. She could easily refuse our bond and, in the end, me.

Another whimper escaped me as I thought of her possible rejection, this one a little louder than the first. Zuri glanced up at me, her brows pulling together.

"Am I hurting you?"

I shook my head, hiding my inner angst, and tightened my arms around her. "No, never. I just don't want to admit our night together is over."

She regarded me a moment before dropping her forehead against my chest. "I know. I don't want to leave you, either."

Inside, I danced a happy jig as my mate revealed her want to be with me. Outside, I pulled her closer and bent to kiss her head again. She hummed her approval.

"The Fates led me to you, Pup. I can feel the connection between us, the thread bonding us. And I trust you, whether that's a smart decision or not." With a huff, she raised her head and looked me in the eyes. "But my coven believes you and your friends are witch hunters."

"We're not." My eyes bore into hers, my face serious.

"I know that. They don't. And they wouldn't believe me when I tried to tell them. They were all certain you were the enemy, and that you tricked me into feeling something for you. As if you worked some kind of mojo over me and voilà— instant witch in your pocket. They were burning black candles last night, for Pete's sake."

It was my turn to look confused. "What do black candles have to do with anything?"

She snorted. "You have a lot to learn about witches."

I rolled us again, ending with her solidly underneath me. Her thighs were still spread around my hips, putting me exactly where I wanted to be…almost. Because as much as my dick was anxious to get to know her better, my mouth was suddenly even more so. Looking down at those eyes, that smile, the way her skin looked so golden against my white sheets—it all made me hungry for her. I was desperate for a taste.

"Will you teach me?" I ran my nose up her neck and under her jaw, inhaling her scent. Her breath stuttered and her pulse flew, making me need to do it again.

"Yes." Her word came out practically on a moan, and I suddenly had the impression we were talking about more than lessons in her heritage. I pulled back slowly, searching out her eyes as my lips rested a breadth away from hers.

"Yes?" I asked once I held her gaze. She nodded but then frowned.

"Morning breath."

I shook my head slowly, not breaking eye contact even as

our noses brushed. "Don't care."

"No?" A smile tugged at the corners of her mouth, revealing a dimple I'd never noticed. Small, almost hidden in her left cheek. I wanted to lick it so bad.

"No." I dropped my head slowly, not wanting to read her wrong or push her too far too fast. But she held my gaze confidently, looking ready. Willing.

"Yes?" I whispered my second request, afraid to disrupt the syrupy anticipation building between us. This was new, so damned new to both of us. One wrong move on my part, and I could destroy it all. I needed to stay slow. Let her decide. Let her lead.

"Yes." She ran her hands up my arms, over my shoulders, and around the back of my neck. Pulling gently, she requested I come closer without asking. I answered her silent plea without pause, stopping when I was close enough to barely feel those lips brushing mine on her inhale. I mouthed *Yes?* one more time, wanting her to be sure, needing her to give her consent before I took us anywhere past where we already were. She gave me the sweetest smile known to man or wolf and a slight head nod.

And then I was lost.

Her lips, soft and warm, pressed against mine. My heart nearly flew out of my chest, and my dick twitched in want of more. Anything more, everything. And when her tongue, her fiery little tongue, ran along the seam of my lips, I knew I could never let her go. One taste, one tiny taste of her, and I was an addict. I wanted her flavor all the time, every day. Wanted to lick every inch of her and see if it changed. Would her neck be tart like fresh raspberries? Her wrist sugary like peaches? Would her nipples be sweet? And just the possibility of getting my tongue anywhere near her pussy had me groaning and rocking my hips against her.

I tangled my tongue with hers, needing more, wanting to plunge and plunder and take ownership. But I held back, as hard as that was. I let her lead me where she wanted to go. As long as she took me with her, I'd follow her to hell and back.

But the kiss, our kiss, was no hell. It was heaven. Pure, sensual heaven. Small licks, sighs, little nibbles on bottom lips…perfection in affection.

Deepening the kiss even further, she wrapped her legs around my thighs and cradled my hips within hers. I wanted to rut—Jesus, did I want to rut—but I held myself as still as I could. I didn't want her to think I was only after a one-sided release. I could wait. She needed a kiss and affection first, a buildup to intimacy. I could happily meet just that need for the next fifty years or so as long as she never stopped running her fingers over my skin or gripping my hair. Okay, maybe not fifty years, the woman was too sexy to hold back that long. At least the next few days. Maybe a week.

Her foot trailed up my calf, her hips angling and pressing against my dick. Fuck, she tasted so good. Felt so perfect. Even holding back for a day suddenly seemed too long.

"Adam." She said my name on a breath, a gasp. I moved my lips to her jawline, desperate for a taste of her skin. "I don't want to, but I really have to go."

I groaned as the flavor of her flesh ignited my taste buds: more savory than sweet, a little spice, and a lot of warmth. I wanted more. Wanted so much, my arms shook as I pulled away from her.

"Okay." I pinched my eyes closed and took a few deep breaths. Calm. I needed to find my calm. Which was going to be really fucking hard with the feel of her soft, hot pussy separated from my dick by only two thin pieces of fabric. I needed to stop thinking about that, pull my hips away from hers, and let her get up.

But as I backed away, she squeezed her legs, pulling my hips into hers, rubbing herself against where I was hard and straining for her. I laughed a cry or cried a laugh; I wasn't sure which. Zuri was killing me, pulling me in and pushing me away at the same time. Giving and taking. Like the pin-up girls painted on the sides of planes during World War Two: topless, smiling, and flipping you off all at the same time. But that thought made me think of seeing Zuri topless, which really wasn't helping the situation.

"Zuri." My voice came out as a plea, as if I were begging. And maybe I was. I was already so fucking hard, I was practically weeping. But I'd stop…of course I'd stop. If only she'd quit grinding on me and making me want to rip her panties down her legs.

She giggled—*giggled!*—as I huffed a laugh and dropped my forehead to her shoulder. I tried to pull away again, but Zuri tightened her legs on me and lifted her hips to slide her covered lips along my dick.

"Fuck, baby. If you need to go, then we have to stop."

She giggled and slid both feet down the backs of my legs and up again, causing goose bumps to rise all over my body. She was quite the tease, my little witch who'd put me under her spell.

"You don't want me to stop," she whispered, all husky and deep and sounding like sex.

I shook my head. "Yeah. I mean no. I mean…dammit."

She pulled me closer, rolling those goddamned hips against me. "I know. I feel it too, the ache to be together. The need for you." She licked my neck, stopping where it curved into my shoulder. I felt her teeth clench against my skin, and that tiny bite made my wolf release a deep and rumbling growl. Zuri moaned and bit me again, obviously delighting in the way my growl deepened at the feel of her teeth on my skin. But then she placed her open mouth against the spot. Hot and wet, she tongued me once, moaned, and finally sucked. Hard.

"Aw, fuck, Zuri." I collapsed on her, my arms shaking as I nearly howled in delight. She was marking me. Fuck yes and please and more and mine, my mate was marking me in a very modern, almost teenage way. Hickeys? I hadn't been given a hickey since I was a fourteen-year-old virgin getting my first hand job in an old hunting blind. But this was nothing compared to that paltry human memory. This was brutal, almost violent in the pressure exerted. She sucked me hard and deep, even capturing my skin between her teeth. And I loved every single moment of it.

My neck burned, the spot where she had attached her mouth sending a steady stream of "oh, fuck yes" to my already aching dick. I pressed her down, rolling my body in a slow slide over hers, rubbing my dick against where she was so hot and wet. Soaked. Enough that even the front of my boxers were wet with her. I loved it, loved knowing I could get her so excited.

On my third press into her, she groaned and released my neck with a wet, popping sound, her eyes coming to meet mine as she smirked.

"Mine."

Her whispered declaration sent my wolf spirit spinning, and I immediately lost what little control I had left. Snarling, I yanked her up the mattress, settling her on her back with my weight firmly on top of her. I gave in to my desire, my need, and ground my hips into hers, rutting against her. She was so hot, so ridiculously wet. I wanted to feel it, taste it, make her come on my tongue. I wanted to slide into that wetness and never leave.

She gasped and wiggled underneath me until I finally pushed against the right spot, the one that made her toes curl and her eyes roll back in her head. Arching, twisting, pulling me closer while trying to push me away at the same time. But I held on, kept up my pace, watched as her body shivered and her chest flushed red.

"Pup."

"Yes," I groaned. Fuck me, she felt so good. I ground against her, hard but cautious, wanting to keep her saying my name that way but not wanting to hurt her. Her head fell back, her mouth falling open as I pressed and pressed and pressed again. So gorgeous, and her pussy felt so good, so soft. I could just imagine how swollen she was getting, how ripe and full and ready for me.

Unable to hold back any longer, I feasted on her body. Collarbone, neck, jaw, ear. I tasted every bit I could reach, wishing for more access, needing to sample every inch. I sucked and licked, even going so far as to bite a few choice spots. Not that she seemed to mind at all.

"So fast, so fast. Fuck, yes," she chanted, moaning and shivering in my hold. I kept moving, my hips finding a rhythm that lifted us both, that made my dick happy and kept her clawing at my shoulders. My balls pulled up tight to my body, that familiar pressure burning low in my belly. I needed her to come; fuck, did I need her to come. Because I was definitely going to.

"Fast, but right," I mumbled before fastening my mouth on her neck and sucking. If she could mark me, I could mark her right back.

She groaned a throaty *oh yes* before sliding a hand between us. With little effort, she reached into the front flap of my boxers, pulling my dick out. I groaned, long and loud, at the feeling of her hand wrapped around me. It made me falter in my rhythm. Not that she seemed to mind. On one thrust, with her hand wrapped firmly around the base of my dick, I pushed against soft cotton, the reduction of the layer of my boxers making me truly feel how wet she was. Her panties were positively soaking. I held still against her, just enjoying the proof of her arousal. But when I went to pull back, she held me still, her fingers slipping under the cotton of her panties to pull them to the side. And then she shifted her hips and placed the head of me exactly where I wanted to be.

With nothing left between me and the sweet heaven of her pussy.

NINE

Azurine

"OH SHIT, ARE YOU sure?" Pup groaned and dropped his head to my chest, shaking with the effort of his restraint. He felt so good in my hand, so hard and thick. I needed to feel him inside me. Craved him in a way that was beyond reason. I knew we were moving too fast, but I didn't want to stop. He had me balancing on a knife's edge, and I was ready to fall.

"Please." I lined him up against me and used my legs to pull him closer. He rolled forward slowly, gently, giving me time to adjust as he slid inside where I was wet and ready for him. His girth stretched me, filling me in a way no other man had before, the rumbling growl vibrating through his body adding more sensation than I ever thought possible. He was going to make me come before he even had a chance to get all the way inside.

On a deep press in, he angled his hips, rubbing against my clit as he did. I groaned, loud and filthy and full-on porn star sounding at how good he felt. How right. How he filled me completely.

"That good, baby? That what you want?" Pup pulled back then pushed in harder, sliding deeper, pressing against my clit again. I couldn't speak, could only clamp my teeth to his neck and claw at his back as he worked his way even farther inside of me.

"So tight. So fucking tight."

His murmurs made me shiver, the sound of his voice over the rumble of his growl unbelievably sexy. I groaned again as his hips finally met mine and he held still, pushing hard against me, stretching me completely.

Ruined. I was forever ruined for any others.

Nothing could compare to how good he felt so deep inside me. Could compare to the slight burn of him stretching me. I throbbed with the pleasure he brought me, muscles already clenching in my need to come, and he'd barely moved.

Unable to hold myself up any longer, I dropped my head back on the mattress and moaned. Pup's lips found mine, his tongue immediately sliding deep into my mouth as he slowly slid back out. My legs shook, my stomach burning with the want to have him back inside me. With a groan, he ended our kiss by biting my bottom lip and smiling against my mouth.

"You're so wet; I can't wait to fuck you with my tongue. But not yet. Fuck, you feel too good wrapped around my dick to stop, no matter how bad I want you to ride my face."

Oh holy Goddess, my sweet, adorable boy had a dirty side. One that made me quiver and crave him even more.

Growling, smirking as if he knew he'd shocked me with his dirty mouth, he thrust into me hard and fast. I squealed in surprise and grabbed hold of his shoulders, clawing his flesh as he repeated the motion again and again. Slamming into me, so fucking deep inside of me. With the way he growled and snarled, the way he gripped my shoulders and pulled me to him on every push, he wasn't just fucking me. He was claiming ownership of my pussy with his body. And I was happy to let him.

"I want more." Pup growled and grabbed my knee, pulling my leg up to his chest and spreading me open for him. The new angle sent shockwaves through my abdomen, making my entire body shake with each thrust.

"Jesus, you're practically sucking me in. My girl likes it deep, don't you? Yeah, I can tell. So wet and soft for me. Fucking perfect home for my dick." Pup grunted and flexed, pushing all the way in only to circle his hips before pulling out. The pressure against my clit was maddening, leading me upward but never quite enough to push me over.

"Please." The moaned plea was all I could say, the pressure inside building to the point of distraction. Nothing mattered except reaching that peak, chasing that pleasure. The world could end and I'd still be begging him to give me more. Thrust harder. Go deeper.

As if reading my mind, Pup pulled completely out of me. Before I could argue, he yanked my panties down my legs and tossed them to the floor. He held my gaze as he grabbed both of my legs and spread me before him. Wide.

"That's better." He kissed my knee before looking down. I should probably have been embarrassed by such a blatant act, knowing I was completely on display for him, but I couldn't find it inside of myself to care. He could look all he wanted as long as he eventually went back to working me over. I was desperate for him. Needy. I wanted him inside of me again.

"So fucking pretty." He hooked my knees over his shoulders then gave me a sweet, almost chaste kiss on the lips as he angled my hips up off the mattress. "Tell me if it's too much."

Spreading me with his arms under my knees, he pushed in slowly. All the way in. So far, my breath caught and my legs locked against his back as a guttural moan left my body. Never had I felt so much. I wanted to die a thousand tiny deaths. I wanted to crawl away from the sudden rush of pleasure-pain.

I wanted to tell him to stop while begging him to go faster. The buildup to what I knew would be a phenomenal orgasm was intense, the pressure growing with every inch of that first downward thrust. And when he was all the way in, seated fully inside with his pubic bone pressing against my clit again, he twisted his hips. My entire body seized as the tip of him hit something inside that'd never been touched, some magical spot that made me moan even louder than before.

"I've got you," he mumbled, squeezing my ass with both hands as he rotated his hips and pulled back. "Never let you go. Never. Just let it come, baby. Give it to me. Want to feel you come. Want it so bad."

Shaking, moaning, clawing, I clung to him as he worked me slow and deep. Over and over he pressed me into the mattress, his weight and his height and his bulk making me feel small and delicate. The sensation only adding to the pleasure building within.

After a few mind-numbing plunges in, he brought his thumb to my lips, pressing inside with a whispered "Suck it." I did as I was told, wrapping my tongue around the digit as best I could. He pulled it from my mouth and trailed his hand down my side, sliding it between us as he reached my hip. And then his lips were on mine, his tongue licking into my mouth with passion and impatience. I responded in kind, the kiss something brutal and rough. He bit my bottom lip hard, making me jump. At the same moment, he pressed his wet thumb against my clit and pushed, pressing the swollen, tender flesh into the bone behind it. I gasped and jumped as he worked his thumb in small circles, never letting up the pressure.

"C'mon, baby. Just a little more. I got you."

One more circle with his thumb and I fell. Long and loud, I called out his name as my body locked up in pleasure. Never had an orgasm lasted so long or felt so good. Never had my muscles seized so completely. They clenched on Pup, pulling him deeper, pulsing around him. Pup didn't ease up on me even as I came. He just kept his hips moving in the same rhythm, kept that thumb pressed against my clit as I throbbed and shook.

"Little more…little more…little…" He thrust harder, faster, two, three more times. But then he faltered, his rhythm breaking as his legs locked and his jaw clenched.

"Fuck, fuck, fuck, Zuri. Fuck." He came with a growl, pressing me into the mattress while his hips continued a jerky, thrusting motion. His head dropped to my chest, even as he pressed himself so very deep inside of me. As his body shook, he kissed the swell of my breast and whispered a quiet "Have to."

And then he bit into my breast.

Pup

OH FUCK.

The words echoed in my head, even as the taste of Azurine's blood sent chills up my spine and I finished coming inside of her. She'd felt so good, so right, and the way her pussy clenched around me as she came had driven me mad. I knew it was wrong to bite her without having discussed what it meant, but I couldn't help myself. Or rather, the wolf instincts took over. Whatever. We'd lost control and bitten our mate without preparing her.

Zuri was going to kill me.

"What the hell, Pup?" Zuri jerked, making my hips push down. My eyes rolled back as my dick got one more good squeeze from her pussy while my teeth were still embedded in her breast. I couldn't focus on her words, could only feel. Her heat, her wetness, the way she squeezed me. My mind was caught in a loop of Zuri's sex. Fuck, she really was going to kill me.

Fighting for clarity, I pulled my mouth off her skin and backed away from her as she struggled to sit up. The movement forced my dick to slide messily from her pussy, the sound positively obscene. It made me want to start all over again. I wasn't kidding when I told her how wet she was. The woman was sloppy, and I loved it. Though being banished from that soft, hot heaven wasn't quite what I wanted at the moment.

"I'm sorry. I didn't mean to do that."

She looked down at the mark on her breast, prodding the flesh with her fingers as she frowned. Watching her fondle her own breasts wasn't helping me calm down. I wanted her again. Wanted her underneath me, on top of me, beside me. Didn't matter. As long as my dick or my fingers or my tongue were in her pussy, I'd be happy.

Damn…the thought of getting my tongue inside her pussy nearly made me whimper in need.

Realizing some kind of mating thrall was warping my reality, I shook off the sex-obsessed thoughts and tried to focus on her face. Tried. My eyes kept darting down to where her fingers brushed against her breast. Where her thumb pressed beside her nipple. Where her—

"That hurt." She looked up at me, an angry almost-pout on her lips.

"I'm sorry." I tried to look her in the eye as I said it, but that thumb was still sitting on the darkened flesh of her nipple. Her tip was pointed and hard and begging me to take it into my mouth. I just wanted a taste. A little lick.

I growled as I fought off the sexual obsession. Zuri's breathing picked up when she heard it, her tongue peeking out to lick her bottom lip. That thumb, the same one that had been captivating me, moved to rub over the hardened peak of her nipple. Once, twice. And then she pinched it.

"Fuck, Zuri." I leapt forward, crashing my lips into hers and plunging my tongue into her mouth. Her arms and legs wrapped around me as I pulled her into my lap. She rocked against me, her wetness making her slide along the length of my quickly hardening dick. But that wasn't what I wanted— not this time.

I wrapped one hand around her waist and pulled her hips up to my chest, letting her upper body fall back to the mattress.

"Pup?"

I shook my head at her breathy question, unable to speak. I needed to taste her. Was dying for it. Absolutely had to know what that amazing pussy felt like against my tongue. I brought her hips up farther, the rest of her body supported by her shoulders on the mattress. I knew she wouldn't be comfortable like that for long, but I didn't intend to make her wait. I needed her to come on my tongue. Immediately.

As soon as I had her legs spread around my shoulders, I dove in, fastening my mouth around her hood and sucking before letting my tongue work its way along the slit. She gasped and shook, her responses leading me down the right path to make her explode. I knew it wouldn't take long, not after the way she'd come when I'd been buried inside her. She was still softly swollen, still wet and ready for more.

I worked my tongue over her clit, pressing hard and flat against her. She moaned and tried to rock her hips, but I had her pinned against me. There was no escaping. Not then, not when I was so desperate to taste her. And taste her I did. Every warm and wet inch of her. I tasted myself on her as well, the thought of the two of us together making me so hard, I nearly came without a single touch.

I knew she was close when she moaned and started trembling. Those signs made me speed up my movements, made me growl against her flesh and slide my teeth along her lips. Her thighs gripped my head, her hands fisting the sheets, until the moment I'd been dying for arrived. With my tongue buried inside of her and my thumb pressed firmly on that bundle of nerves I wanted to get even more acquainted with, she came with a moan I was sure half the state could hear. My wolf preened at the thought, knowing all the other males around would hear how much pleasure I gave my mate and stay away. She was mine. Forever.

As she loosened the grip her thighs had on my head, I slowly dropped her bottom half back to the mattress. The girl was jelly, which made me want to pound on my chest and grunt. I'd done that to her; I'd made her look like that. The man and the wolf both liked knowing we could make our mate that happy.

She sighed and gave me a dopey grin, looking like a woman well and truly sated. I curled up next to her, ready to spend a little time just enjoying the feeling of her flesh against mine. But then she glanced over my shoulder.

"Shit, is that the time?" Before I could answer, she was out of bed and pulling her clothes on. "I've got to get back to the house."

Panic settled over me like a blanket of ice. I had to talk to her; she had to know what the bite meant. "Wait…you're leaving?"

"I know; it's supershitty of me. There's a lot going on with my coven and this wolf issue, so I don't know when I can come back. Probably not today." She rushed over, thighs pressing against the side of the mattress as she leaned to place a soft kiss against my lips. "Thanks for letting me stay the night. And everything else. I owe you big time, though I doubt I'll bite you the way you did me."

She gave me a saucy smile as she pulled her sweatshirt over her head, and then she was out the door. I sat in a stunned stupor, my chin still wet with her juices and my mind a tangled mess.

I bit her.

How did I let this happen? I'd been so careful, so completely focused on her so I didn't push her too hard. Everything we'd done, we'd done because I was absolutely certain it was what she wanted. Until the bite.

The bite was a mistake. Not one I regretted, exactly. She was my mate. Of course I wanted to link us with a claiming bite. But she had no clue what that small tear of flesh meant. And when I should have been talking to her, telling her exactly what I'd done, I'd let my libido run the show and tongue-fucked her instead. Brilliant.

She had no idea I'd marked her for eternity. No clue she would smell like me to any other shifters she came across. She didn't yet know how her aging would slow down, her body moving into stasis so we could live extended lives together.

And she had absolutely no clue how she'd broken my heart when she'd told me she wouldn't bite me back.

TEN

Azurine

I BOUNDED THROUGH THE woods, unable to control the smile on my face. Pup was everything I could have ever asked for. Strong, gorgeous, loving, kind…everything. The way he let me decide how far and how fast we went physically without making me beg or plead or even ask for what I wanted was so refreshing. The way he kept whispering the question "Yes?" and how he watched me, those things drove me wild with need for him. It was such a turn-on after dealing for years with men who always put their own wants ahead of mine. No, not men. Pup was a man. Those previous lovers were just boys.

But my connection to him was more than lust. I knew it, could feel the bond in my heart. He was someone I could trust, someone I could give my heart to. We could have a wonderful future together. If only.

Because as I hurried away from the man consuming my thoughts and toward the lighthouse, my happiness faded and anxiety took hold. My coven, my family, was not accepting of him. I needed to do some major damage control and figure out a way to make my sister understand how Pup was fated to be mine. He was the end to my red thread, the other half to my soul. I needed him in my life like I needed air or water or magick. There simply wasn't an option to not have him.

It would take time, that I knew, but I hoped to somehow convince the coven of his trustworthiness. I needed them to know he wasn't a witch hunter. Starting with Amber. With my both my sisters on my side, I knew the rest of the coven would come around. They had to.

I snuck into the house through the back door, sidestepping the stacks of pots and cauldrons in the mudroom. I could hear the voices of some of my covenmates coming from the greenhouse, but I wasn't ready to see them. I needed to clean up before I went to help them with the protection spells. While being shunned by them had been beyond painful, I knew helping protect our home would work in my favor. If I could show them how I hadn't changed, how I was still the same girl they'd always known, they might give me a chance once it was time to bring up Pup again. I just had to have hope and faith.

I hurried up the back stairs and down the hall to my bedroom, thankful for the clear path into the safety of my room. But as I closed the door behind me, I realized—too late—that I wasn't alone.

"I hoped you'd be smart enough to sneak home before dawn, but apparently not. What took you so long?"

I turned and met the appraising gaze of Scarlett, who was lounging across my bed. Her eyes lit up as she took in what must have been my total walk-of-shame style. No shoes, pants wrinkled, sweatshirt—I glanced down at myself—yep, on backward. I was a walking billboard for Just Got Fucked 'R Us. I coughed unnecessarily and ran a hand over my hair, nearly cringing at how tangled it felt.

"Hey." I paused, uncomfortably unsure what to do next. Scarlett smirked and raised an eyebrow at me. The brat. I rolled my eyes and hurried toward my dresser as if it was perfectly normal to walk into my room after spending the night with a sexy shapeshifter who practically made me stop breathing with the way he touched me.

"You look like one hell of a happy woman."

I shrugged and bit back a grin. What could I say, the boy had skills.

"Did anyone notice I was gone? I know there's a group here for the protection spells."

"Yeah, the old biddies are digging in the dirt again. As if soil and iron are all we need to hunt a hunter." She stood and strolled in a circle around me. Assessing. Inspecting. Making me feel like a criminal on trial. But she wouldn't get me to crack.

"So, how's your new pet?"

I huffed and rolled my eyes. "He's not my pet. But he's fine. Good. Fine. Better than fine. He's…great, really."

Fuck…busted.

Scarlett laughed. "Damn, girl. You rode him like a jockey at the Preakness, didn't you?"

My cheeks burned as I scurried into the en suite bathroom. "That's not really your business."

Her laugh only grew.

"Yeah, yeah, yuck it up." I flipped her off and kept walking. "You're just jealous you were here all alone while I was otherwise occupied."

I closed the door to the bathroom and leaned against it, giving in to the need to just…grin. I felt good, giddy even. My body, my heart, my brain, the magickal core inside of me. Every ounce of me felt balanced and complete. It was a good feeling, rapturous almost. It was as if I'd discovered something I hadn't even realized was missing from my life. And maybe I had…in Pup.

"By the way," Scarlett whisper-yelled through the closed

door, making me jump. "You might want to shower and find a turtleneck. You reek of eau de mangy-mutt, and it's going to be superhard to explain the hickeys."

I immediately checked out my reflection in the mirror, my eyes going to the red marks decorating my neck. Wonderful. I yanked my sweatshirt over my head and gasped. I'd almost forgotten the way Pup had bitten me. But there was no forgetting it now—the teeth marks Pup left behind were obvious. They looked brutal. Possibly even worse than the hickeys he'd left up and down my neck. Scarlett was right… I'd need to cover them with clothing because none of my makeup would fix them.

Leaning over the counter, I examined the bite on my breast. It didn't hurt. It was warm and something I definitely noticed, but it wasn't painful. Even if it looked like it should be.

Curious, I brought my hand up to get a better feel for the mark. As I ran my fingers over the edge of the raised crescent, a deep pulse of arousal exploded through me. I did it again, this time brushing the length of it, and nearly lost my balance. Whatever the mark was, it was not a simple bite from a lover. Some kind of energy was wrapped around it, something warm and intriguing. I'd have to ask Pup about it the next time we were alone. See if the bite worked for him the way it did for me. If his touch would cause the same deep, explosive arousal.

By the Gods, if it worked the same way for him, the two together might just actually kill me. Death by orgasm. Damn.

Knowing Scarlett was still just on the other side of the door, I pushed those thoughts aside and turned away from the mirror. "Thanks, Scar."

"Anytime, Zuri. That's what sisters are for. To help keep you from getting into trouble. Just hurry up. We need to get downstairs and start working on getting the biddies to give up this ridiculous shunning."

"My thoughts exactly."

TWENTY MINUTES LATER, I rushed down the stairs with my wet hair braided into pigtails and a turquoise turtleneck sweater covering the evidence of my night. I was ready to face the coven, ready to begin the process of regaining their support, even though something dark and angry swirled in my gut. I had the strongest urge to go back to the camp where Pup was staying. To be closer to him. But I couldn't risk it. If the coven found out, I'd be in even more trouble than I already was.

I resettled a smile on my face as I reached the greenhouse, ready to offer my help with the protection spells. The room was humid as always, windows foggy as the heat and cold met through the panes of glass. Amber stood at the far corner, frowning at Clara Gardner as she and Bethesda worked different additives into bushels of soil. Sarah sat in a chair in the corner, looking pale and tired as she huddled under a blanket. Seeing her so obviously sick was a kick to the gut, one that filled me with guilt. I should have been spending time with her, not playing house with Pup. No matter how right it felt when I was with him. She was the only mother I'd ever known, and I was losing her to the Summerlands. No amount of comfort or care from another should compete with what she needed from me.

Shame swamped me, pulled me under its devastating wave. I had spent the night in bed with a man while Sarah suffered alone.

"Stop it," Scarlett whispered, surprising me with her very presence.

"Stop what?"

"I can practically feel the guilt radiating from you. Sarah was fine; I checked on her multiple times last night. I would've called you if she'd needed you."

I sighed, not really feeling better. "I owe you one."

"Bitch, you owe me like twelve. Now go say hi." She smiled as she walked over to a couple of women burning a pile of something dark and rootlike.

I was hurrying across the room on my way over to talk with Sarah when Clara hissed.

"How dare you?"

The entire room went silent in a blink. Sarah's eyes met mine, showing concern for a moment before a deep sadness washed over her. A sadness directed at me. Dreading what I would see, I turned to face Clara, ignoring the stares of the rest of the coven. I knew whatever was wrong was about me. Felt it. Things were about to get ugly.

When I finally saw the ancient witch's glare directed at me, I took a step back. "Pardon me?"

Bethesda stepped from around the older witch, a scowl on her face. "Where have you been, Weaver?"

I glanced around the room, catching the shocked expression on Amber's face. "I'm not sure what you mean. I was just upstairs."

Bethesda strode my way, a fire burning in her ebony eyes. "Don't twist my words. I know you were with those witch hunters."

She tilted her head and examined me, going so far as to sniff the air around me. "What did you do? Lay with one of them? Did you use your water magick to entice once of those mongrels into having sex with you?"

"I don't…I'm not sure…" I caught Scarlett's eyes, knowing mine had to be wide with panic. *How could they know?*

"You're not sure if you spent the evening with your new pet? How convenient." Bethesda spun and addressed the silent witches around the room. "Ladies, we must take a stand. Azurine Weaver has brought danger deep within our coven. She's lied to us, invited in the evil that hunts us, and has lain with one of them in her effort to undermine our union. We cannot allow this type of deceit. Already we've shunned her, and less than twelve hours later, she stands before us, reeking of witch hunter."

Amber stepped from behind Bethesda, her face a mess of pain and confusion. "Sarah is dying, the coven is scattering in fear, and you betrayed us for a man? How could you, Zuri?"

"No." I reached for my sister, silently willing her to give me a chance to explain. But that chance would never come. My heart broke as she pulled away from me. I looked around the room, feeling small and vulnerable in the face of the angry looks being sent my way. "I would never betray this coven. The men in the camp south of here are not witch hunters. They're wolf shifters, but they're not a threat. They're not here for us, nor are they a danger to our coven. The Fates led me there—"

"Do not disrespect the Fates with your untruths." Bethesda stormed my way, her eyes positively blazing. "You have all borne witness to this witch's lies and the danger she brings us. Our coven is being hunted, and yet she goes to the ones who would kill us all. She cavorts with them. She spreads her legs for them."

My face burned and my heart raced, but I had no idea what to say. I *had* slept with Pup, but I knew he and his friends weren't a danger to us. Unfortunately, Bethesda had just branded me not only a whore but also a willful betrayer of the coven. And while I knew neither of those was true, convincing the coven of my innocence seemed completely out of reach.

"I call for an immediate and binding vote." Bethesda stepped to the middle of the room and raised her hands in the air. "Goddess of Light, Mother of the Earth, we call on your guidance to show us the way. Let the element of air bring us sight and wisdom as we evaluate the actions of one of your daughters."

Amber swirled her hand over her head, causing a biting wind to spin through the greenhouse. I shivered and curled in on myself as other witches exclaimed their shock over the sudden drop in temperature. But not Bethesda. She stood strong, hands raised, eyes closed. For several seconds, nothing happened. The wind blew itself out and the temperature once again rose, but no one moved. No one spoke.

Until Bethesda dropped her hands and nodded. "I have seen the path we must take."

She circled the room, looking each of my covenmates in the eyes as she passed. Even Sarah, who shook her head with tears in her eyes but said nothing, making my stomach drop in fear. And when Bethesda was finished, when she'd completed her circle and made contact with every witch besides me, she pulled her crystal talisman from around her throat. The stone in the middle was a deep indigo azurite, the color used for centuries in the pursuit of spiritual guidance and divination. Bethesda held the talisman like an offering, lifting it high in the air.

"Coven of Parity Lake, I call for a full banishing of Azurine Weaver."

As witches gasped around the room, Bethesda dropped the talisman to the floor. It landed with a sickening crunch, sparks flying. Bethesda picked it up and held it aloft once more, high enough for the entire room to see. The witches around me murmured excitedly as they saw the results—the stone had lightened to a shade of purple that made my stomach drop. The color represented spiritual guidance and contact with the spirits. It also was the color we used when driving away evil.

Bethesda made sure each witch in the room saw the way the stone had changed color before slipping it back around her neck.

"The spirits have spoken. We must banish the evil that Azurine Weaver represents. Who here supports this decision with the guidance of the Goddess?"

The silence was a physical being, something wet and heavy

in the room. No one had been banished from the coven in over two hundred years. It was the worst the coven could do to a witch, sending her out in the world alone without her fellow witches to help strengthen her magick. It also meant being cut off from all of her family and friends.

And by the way the hands were being raised around the room, the coven was united in my banishment.

"I do not support the banishment of this girl, Bethesda." Sarah's voice sounded rough and scratchy, but there was a strength to it no one could deny. "If Azurine says the Fates called her to this man, then I believe her. Perhaps we should investigate them further before we make such a rash decision."

Bethesda looked around the room at the hands in the air, ignoring the way some of them fell at Sarah's words. "The decision has been made. Pack your belongings, Azurine. You're no longer welcome on coven land."

I looked to Sarah in fear. She'd always been there for me, always been able to patch up whatever I'd broken. But by the sadness on her face and the tears running down her cheeks, this was more than she could repair. This was something she could not rescue me from, and that reality turned my blood cold.

Scarlett came to stand by me, her face ablaze with fury and her fingertips glowing as she held her elemental power close.

"What about the protection spells? The hunter? We need Zuri's magick."

Bethesda shook her head. "The coven is to leave here, immediately. If anyone chooses to stay"—she glanced at Sarah—"it's at their own risk."

"So we run, and we leave a sick, old woman to what? Die alone? Defend herself against a hunter? How can you be so callous to the woman who's led our coven for years." Scarlett's eyes practically glowed, her inner fire too close to the surface. "I've met the man who claims Zuri as his mate, and I believe her when she says he's not a hunter. I sat at their camp for hours without a single trace of fear or wariness telling me they were a danger. And I believe my sister when she says the Fates pulled her to him."

She looked around the room, staring particularly hard at our sister who stood in the back with her hand still raised against me. "We all saw her yesterday afternoon, those of us with even the slightest gift of empathy knew of her emotional unsteadiness. Did you forget? Did you disregard what you saw and felt?" She caught our sister's eyes, glaring hard. "How dare you not believe your own sister? How dare you pull the only family she's ever known away from her at a time when we need to come together to usher Sarah to the Summerlands? You send your sister into the woods where a hunter lies in wait, and for what? Having sex with the man whom the Fates drew her to?"

"He's a hunter," Amber said, her voice small but solid.

"He is not a hunter! Yes, he's a wolf shifter, but he is not a witch hunter." Sparks flew as Scarlett yelled, small drops of liquid fire falling from her fingertips, making the rest of the witches in the room back away. "You're all too afraid to see how stupid you're being. We have the Goddess on our side; we have magick. If there truly is a witch hunter, let's bring him the witches. He'd be dead before nightfall if we would only fight back instead of hiding and running."

"We can't attack him without cause. An it harm none, do what ye will," Amber countered.

Scarlett glowered at our oldest sister. "This entire coven just broke the Rede by banishing one of its members without cause."

"Your loyalty to your sister, while fascinating in its ignorance, has nothing to do with this case." Bethesda faced me, her gaze strong as it held mine. "Azurine, go pack your things. Our decision is final."

I nodded and dropped my gaze to the floor. Heat flooded my cheeks and my heart ached in my chest. This was it, my last moments with the people who'd been my family since I was born. The only family I'd ever known.

Scarlett's overheated hand stopped me as I stepped toward the door. When I looked up at her, she was staring at Amber.

"The Weaver sisters are a unit. A triad." Scarlett took two steps toward Amber and held out the hand not holding mine. "Are you standing with your sisters today?"

Amber stood silent and still for a moment before slowly shaking her head. That one movement, that tiny side-to-side motion, was more cutting than anything else that had happened in the greenhouse.

Scarlett's hair began to glow at the ends, a sure sign her rage was quickly burning out of control. "Fine. You want to abandon your sisters when they need you, go ahead. But don't think we'll ever forget this."

Scarlett took a deep breath—the only outward sign of her fear—and tightened her hold on my hand. Her skin burned me, but I didn't let go. We were stronger together. All witches were stronger with others of their kind around them, but Scarlett and I truly were a matched set. And right at that moment, I felt as if she was the only thing holding me together.

"I'm going with my sister." Scarlett lifted her chin and glared at each coven member, one by one. "You have broken the Wiccan Rede, you have banished a woman who did nothing but follow the path the Fates told her to, and you have endangered every member of this coven by failing to listen to us as we informed you of your misguided certainty of where the threat lies. I swear upon my mother's grave, the man Azurine has taken as her soul mate is no hunter."

Gasps echoed through the room again, including my own. Swearing upon the dead was a strong promise, a heavy responsibility that no one took lightly. Scarlett had just proclaimed, at the cost of her own death for a lie, that what she knew was fact. That I was being truthful. My sister had thrown the full weight of her support behind me, and I'd never been more grateful for her.

The faces around us went from surprise to anger, the looks this time focused on Bethesda Marrin. But it was too late. My fate had been set, and only a full tribunal refusal or an overturning of coven power could negate my banishment.

And deep down, I didn't know if I wanted it turned over. Not after the way they'd shattered my trust in them.

Scarlett and I moved as one toward the door. But my sister wasn't finished. She always had been the one to turn that final screw in an argument.

"You all disappoint me, you disappoint our ancestors, and you disappoint the Goddess. May your action weigh heavily on your soul, and the rule of three be upheld in the coming days."

And with that, we exited the greenhouse, hand in hand. Probably for the last time.

ELEVEN

THE FREEZING RAIN STARTED in the early morning hours. The ground quickly turned dark and soupy, the areas with an existing buildup of mud turning near-white with frost. Heavy and pounding, the water washed away the dirt and the debris that had accumulated since the last downpour. I sat on the porch of my cabin, drinking coffee and wishing a simple rain shower could wash away my own sins as easily.

"So Beast thinks Spook isn't our guy?" Rebel asked, leaning back in his chair in a way that would have sent me crashing to the floor as a kid.

"Yeah. I'm going to drive down there in a bit, see what's up with the crew. Maybe something will kick off my instincts." I bent forward, planting my elbows on my knees and resting my head in my hands. "It's only like an hour and a half to get down there. Figure a day to hang, and I'll be back by morning. It's nothing."

"You know I can give you a break if you need it, man. You just found your mate yesterday—"

"No." I turned my head in time to see Rebel's lip curl. "No disrespect, but you gave me a job to do, and I will get it done.

Meeting Azurine won't get in the way of my responsibilities."

Rebel watched me for a few long minutes, assessing and inspecting as I expected him to do. I held my position, not looking away, making sure he knew exactly how serious I was about this. I'd earn my place, no matter what.

Finally, he nodded his acceptance. "Okay then." He leaned back in his chair again, rocking gently while looking past the muddy clearing and over to the trees. "Just know that the offer stands. There are other guys who can investigate this for me. And I fully respect the Rites of Klunzad. I'd be more than happy to set up a team to guard the camp should you choose to complete your mating the traditional way."

Shame stealing some of the volume of my voice, I murmured, "I kind of already completed the mating, sort of."

Rebel stopped his rocking, looking serious as he turned to me. "What do you mean, sort of?"

I choked on a sigh, practically ready to bang my head on the railing at my own stupidity. "I bit her."

The front legs of Rebel's chair hit the floor. "You're fucking joking."

"Nope. I just…lost control while we were…" I glanced his way and gave him a "you know" look. He raised his eyebrows at me.

"So you performed the claiming bite during…coitus."

I sat back in my chair. "It's the twenty-first century, man. I bit her during sex, not coitus."

Rebel smacked me upside the back of my head with a growl. "Fine, you smartass. Let's just be blunt; you bit her while fucking." He huffed as I cringed. "Did you even ask her if she wanted to be bonded that way? Did you explain what it means?"

I ducked my head and whispered a regretful "No."

"That's what I thought." Rebel ran a hand over his face and

groaned. "What are you gonna do?"

"I have to tell her. She's going to be pissed as hell, but I can't keep it from her. I didn't mean to this morning, I just got… distracted."

Rebel snorted. "Yeah, we all heard you being distracted. Nice job, by the way."

"Sorry," I said, embarrassed and yet…not. I frowned as he pulled his phone from his pocket. "What're you doing?"

"Trying to figure out who I can call in for the K-zoo den issue."

I sat up straighter, my neck burning as my heart raced. "No way, man. I can do this."

Rebel shook his head, still staring at his phone. "I know you can, but you need to focus on Azurine right now."

"Rebel." My whispered plea stopped him, bringing his attention back to me. "I don't want to fail again. Let me do the job. I can find out who stole the money and still deal with my mate."

He put his phone down, turning that intense, Alpha stare on me and not letting me look away. "I did this, remember? My mate left me hours after I found her, and I suffered through it for months. Don't be stupid like I was. No one, not a single Breed brother, would blame you or think less of you if you needed to take some time away to deal with the mating. You have nothing to prove."

I turned enough so he could see the back of my jacket, the bare expanse of leather where I dreamed of a growling wolf insignia.

"I have everything to prove, man."

Once again, he watched me, silently weighing me against some measure in his head. And then he gave me a head nod.

"All right. I can respect the need to earn it. But know this, if you need it, the time's yours. No questions, no shame, and no loss of respect."

"Understood." I nodded once. While the offer of time off was one I would've loved to take advantage of, I couldn't. I had to focus on the long-term, which meant earning my patch. Without that, I was nobody. Nothing. Not even close to good enough for someone like my Azurine.

We sat in silence for a few minutes, both of us watching the rain, lost in our own thoughts. Mine revolved around Zuri, around the bond I could feel between us. There was a staticky feeling to it, as if it were a radio station I was just out of range for.

Trying to ignore the sense of panic slowly gnawing a hole in my gut at the idea of Azurine being outside of my reach, I slouched in my chair.

"You tell Charlotte yet about the whole biting shit?"

He sighed. "Not all of it yet. We're just getting solid, you know? We're finally talking about the future of our relationship. She's even considering us moving in together."

"That's awesome, man."

"Yeah." He grinned but then forced it back as he watched the rainfall. "I'm worried that telling her about the slower aging thing will put her over the edge. It's like the whole 'Hey, we'll live for centuries together if I bite you, but you'll have to watch your brother die a human death' might be the straw that breaks the camel's back. I don't know if she'd choose to stay with me in that situation."

I shrugged. "No way to know until you ask."

His head whipped in my direction and he growled. "See if it's so easy when you have to tell your little witch that not only is she now bonded to you for eternity and that you can feel her presence no matter where she goes, but that you did it without her knowledge or consent."

My chest and neck burned, reminding me of my human

youth when I'd been scolded or corrected for doing something wrong. The embarrassment of knowing how much I'd screwed up. And I had definitely done something wrong this time.

"I couldn't stop myself." I coughed, trying to clear the lump growing in my throat. Fuck, I'd screwed up bad. Shaking my head, I whispered, "Everything came down to my teeth meeting her skin. There was nothing else in the entire world. And I hate it, but I couldn't stop."

We sat in silence again; the only sound the dance of the rain as it hit the ground. But then Rebel sighed.

"Yeah, I know what you mean." Rebel leaned back in his chair, rocking and balancing on two legs again. "It's not easy to hold back on that particular instinct. I struggle with it every time."

"You do?" I asked. Rebel was a master at control, always so focused. At least until he met Charlotte. His struggling in anything wolf-related was a surprise.

"Sure. But I'm a lot older than you, both as a man and a wolf. Control comes with time." He stiffened as he looked out toward his cabin, once again dropping his chair back to four legs. "And it looks like our time is up."

Charlotte hurried our way with a jacket over her head to keep from getting wet. Not that it helped. She was soaked within seconds. Beast followed behind her, grinning and tilting his head back to catch the rain.

"Sometimes I think you've got a little Labrador in you, my friend," Rebel called to Beast as he met Charlotte at the steps. He grinned and kissed her, his hands sliding down to grip her hips. "Hello, mate."

"Hi." She looked my way as Rebel led her back to his chair, pulling her onto his lap once he sat down. "What are you two boys doing over here? Plotting world domination?"

I chuckled. "No, just talking about women."

"Oh. Your Elizabeth Taylor lookalike got you all riled up?" Charlotte asked with a smile.

"My what?"

She rolled her eyes. "Azurine. The girl looks just like Elizabeth Taylor in her younger days."

"That's why she looks familiar." Beast shook his head. "It's been driving me crazy."

Rebel pulled Charlotte closer, his hand resting high on her thigh. "No matter who she looks like, Pup here needs to figure out how to go about wooing her. He'll be miserable without his mate."

Charlotte ran her fingers through his hair and leaned over to kiss his forehead. When she moved back, he met her gaze, both of them smiling subtly. The amount of love between the two of them was obvious in that look. Soft and filled with emotion, both their faces reflected the adoration they felt for one another. I pulled my phone from my pocket and snapped a quick picture. Rebel looked over with a furrowed brow at the click, earning a shrug from me.

"For later."

He didn't look any less confused, but I had no interest in explaining why I'd needed to capture the look they'd shared. I doubted I could explain it to myself.

"Do you think she'll come back today?" Charlotte asked, turning on Rebel's lap to face me. "The rain sucks, but maybe she has a car."

"I don't know. I didn't get a chance—"

The static stopped. I waited, looking out toward where I knew Zuri lived, waiting for something. Anything.

"Pup?" Rebel sounded concerned, but I just shook my head. I needed to concentrate. To wholly focus on my bond. Something was happening, but I didn't know what it was.

A sudden tug at my heart had me on my feet, a throaty

rumble in my chest.

"What's going on, Pup?" Beast asked as he came to stand by my side.

I shook my head, too consumed with the pull to my mate to answer. Emotions like I'd never known swirled around me. Fear, pain, loss, desperation…but they weren't mine. Something was very, very wrong with Azurine.

I growled louder as her pain increased, my bond to her coming in loud and clear. The railing snapped under my hands as I gripped it. My growl grew louder, my mind going dark as pain like I'd never experienced grew, swelled, overtook my heart…

Rushed toward me.

"What's happening?" Charlotte asked, her small voice coming from behind me.

Closer, closer, closer…the heartbreak swelled within me, outside of me, all around me. "She's coming."

Rebel and Charlotte came to stand on my right as Beast flanked me on my left. A deep, dark pit of emotion was headed my way, sliding along the bond between the two of us. Damn, how could she be dealing with that level of hurt? How could she even function under the weight of that much pain?

Two shadows appeared through the falling sleet.

"Oh shit." Charlotte's words barely registered as I jumped off the porch and raced toward Azurine and her sister. Both girls were soaking wet, shivering in the near-winter rain while holding a single suitcase each.

"What's wrong?"

Zuri looked up, her eyes meeting mine for only a second before my heart died. The sadness on her face was a physical weight, pulling me into a pit of emotion alongside her. Pain like I'd never experienced lived in those jade eyes. Pain that was ripping her apart. I wrapped my arms around her, wishing I could shield her from whatever was making her hurt so horribly.

As soon as I had her pressed against me, she broke into sobs. Shoulders shaking, she cried into my chest as my stomach dropped. I looked over her head to her sister, almost panicking at the collapse of my mate. But Scarlett was no immediate help. She seemed more angry than sad.

"What happened?" Charlotte asked as she joined us in the freezing rain.

Scarlett shrugged. "The old biddies kicked her out. You got any whiskey?"

"What do you mean, they kicked her out?" Charlotte asked.

Scarlett shrugged. "They banished Zuri for sleeping with the enemy. I'm pretty much along for the ride."

Beast appeared beside her, grabbing both girls' bags and directing Scarlett around us.

"C'mon, Smokey. I'm sure between Rebel and me, we've got enough whiskey to light your fire."

Scarlett snorted. "I can light my own fires, thank you very much. Or do I need to give you another demonstration?"

As they left, I gripped Zuri tighter, bending my body over hers, trying to shield her as best I could from the rain.

When the sobs lessened enough that I thought she could speak, I kissed the top of her head and asked, "What happened?"

"They knew."

Her mumbled words made no sense, but I didn't question her on them. Instead, I waited for her to continue, to help me understand.

"They knew I'd been with you. They said they could smell the hunter on me. Which is crazy because you're not a hunter." She paused, shaking in my arms. When she spoke next, the tone of her voice tore a hole right through my heart. "I don't understand what happened."

My heart sank as my eyes dropped to where my teeth marks

would surely be visible if not for the sweater she wore. They smelled me on her—not on her, in her—because my wolf essence now ran through her blood, slowing her aging and working as a homing signal for me to find her.

"I'm so sorry." I wanted to tell her what I'd done, how all of this was my fault, but I couldn't get the words out. I could blame the betrayal of my family on their own actions, but this one was all me. It was my fault Zuri was hurting the way she was.

"I have no place to go." Her broken whisper crushed my heart into a lump of sand.

I swallowed hard, buried in guilt and shame. "You'll stay with me. You can always stay with me."

She shook her head. "We barely know each other."

"Then you can stay with Rebel and Charlotte. Or we'll open up one of the empty cabins for you and Scarlett until we figure out what to do." I pulled back to look into those beautiful eyes again, fighting to keep my hands from shaking. "You'll never not have a place to go. We're mates, threads tied to one another. I'll always make sure you have a home."

She stared at me, all wide eyes and rain-slicked face, looking so beautiful even in her pain. Then she nodded.

"Okay."

"Okay." I swallowed the bile rising in my throat at the thought of telling her how horribly I'd fucked things up. "Is that 'Okay, open up a cabin' or 'Okay, I'll stay with you'?"

She smiled for the first time since she walked into camp. "Okay, I'll stay with you. Though we should probably open a cabin for Scarlett, unless you plan on sharing the room with more than one Weaver sister."

Leaning down, I pulled her close and placed a soft kiss to her lips. "There's only one Weaver sister I want with me. Scarlett's on her own."

TWELVE

"SO YOUR PARENTS ARE still alive?" I walked across the room, drying my hair with a towel. A hot shower and some food in my stomach had done me good; I no longer felt as if my world was ending. Though being around Pup could've had something to do with that. The man exuded a calm that I craved.

"Yeah, and they live not too far from here."

"But you don't want to go see them."

He shrugged. "They think I'm dead."

I froze, towel still wrapped around my hair as I stared at him. "What?"

Pup leaned back, finally full after eating almost two large pizzas on his own. "When a human becomes a shifter, their aging slows. I'm ten years into my new life and still look like the kid who supposedly died in a car crash." He broke my gaze, looking to the floor. "Besides, they wouldn't want to see me."

His last sentence hit me as if it were a physical blow, the force knocking me a step back. "What parents wouldn't want to at least see their kid?"

"The parents who kicked that kid out of the house when

he was fifteen." Pup stood, looking angry for the first time. He took two steps toward me before coming to an abrupt stop and putting both hands in his hair. "Zuri, you have to understand. I didn't have the Kool-Aid childhood. Neither of my parents were what you'd call involved. And when they decided I was old enough to be on my own, they sent me out on my own. No help, no making sure I had a place to go, nothing. If I hadn't been working for Beast at the time, I don't know what I would've done. Besides, I'd been out of touch with them for five years before the accident that Beast used to fake my death. I doubt they miss me."

I waited for him to calm down, not wanting to upset him more than he already was. It didn't take long. Within a few seconds, he dropped his arms and cracked his neck. Once he took a deep breath and his shoulders relaxed, I once again started pulling the water from my hair.

And I remained silent.

His story and mine had a similarity that made my chest hurt and my eyes burn. Both abandoned by the family we relied on, both struggling with knowing they didn't want us. But in his case—for that betrayal to have happened so young— it was a devastation I wondered if he'd ever get over. When he was kicked out, he had nothing but Beast. For me, all I had was Scarlett.

But now, Pup and I had each other.

I didn't feel the need to acknowledge his anger; it was a natural reaction to something that must have hurt him so much. Pup had a different opinion, though, because he came over and kissed my forehead as if in apology. When he pulled away, the look on his face screamed regret, but I ignored it. There was nothing to be sorry about.

Reaching out, I offered him the comfort of my touch with a hand on his arm. "So Beast is like a father figure to you."

"No, not father." He brought my hand up to his lips, kissing the back and giving me a small smile that made my heart flutter. "Maybe big brother or uncle. He took me in when I had no one. He taught me a trade and made sure I had a roof over my head and a full belly at night. That's more than my parents did, but he never tried to tell me what to do. He's always let me make my own mistakes."

His expression turned guilty, making me wonder what he was about to say next. But he said nothing, just turned to walk back toward the bed. When he settled himself on the mattress, he had that same look on his face as he worried his lip. I hung my towel from the door handle and joined him, almost afraid to know what was on his mind. I sat at the opposite end of the bed and tangled my legs with his.

"I'm glad you found Beast and that he was there when you needed him."

"Me too." He grabbed my foot and tugged, forcing me closer. With his eyes on mine, he began massaging my foot. Pressing, sliding, running his fingers over my flesh. "My life before wasn't easy—it's still not quite sunshine and daisies—but I'm happy. I have my friends in the Feral Breed, I have my bike, and I have a lot of freedom."

He tugged again, this time directing my legs around his hips and pulling me up to straddle his lap. I stayed pliant, forcing him to work to get me where he wanted. Not that he needed to. I'd happily snuggle into his warm body for the next month if he let me. He was the only thing keeping the pain of the last few hours at bay.

Once Pup had me firmly on his lap, he sighed and pulled me into a deep hug. Arms and legs wrapped around each other, hips and chests and stomachs pressed tight. It was the epitome of a cuddle; soft, warm, and blissful. We stayed that way for several minutes, simply enjoying the press of one body against the other.

Eventually, our hands stopped being still, sliding underneath the fabric covering us to meet the skin we each seemed to crave. Goose bumps broke out over my body as Pup's thick fingers pressed into the muscles of my back, and he sighed as I ran my fingers over his shoulders and up into his hair.

"I come from nothing," he whispered. "I've always had nothing." Pup ran his hands up my arms as he nuzzled the length of my nose with his. "But now I have you. I just…I really hope I get to keep you."

I breathed a laugh. "I kind of have nowhere to go. You're stuck with me, at least for now."

He stilled, breathing harshly. My heart dropped as doubts and fears crept into my mind. He'd been so back-and-forth all morning, as if happy to see me but regretful about something. Maybe he didn't want me to stay with him, maybe he wished I would have told him no when he asked.

With a suddenness that made me jump, he gripped my shoulders from behind and pressed his lips to mine, sliding his tongue along the seam until I opened for him. The kiss was deep but gentle, soft and powerful in a way that made my breath catch and my heart explode. The emotions behind it were strong, the need and fear he shared with me obvious. And when he was done, when he'd made me a wobbly mess of girl-flesh in his lap, he pulled back and licked his lips.

"Sorry," he whispered. "I'm so, so sorry."

Fear. It pulled me under, dragging me into a sea of doubt. "For what? Pup, what's wrong?"

He shook his head, not meeting my gaze. I arched back to pull myself from his hold, but he tightened his grip, his eyes desperate as they met mine. He whispered my name, once, so quiet it was almost silent. I tilted my head, clinging to him, too afraid to ask him what was wrong a second time. Slow and cautious, he leaned down and recaptured my lips, this time keeping the kiss shallow and soft until he pulled away with a sigh.

"I'm an idiot, for a lot of reasons." He pulled back, his eyes a fiery green even as his smile looked a little forced. "I'm talking too much. You know all the dark and dirty of my past. Tell me yours."

His slight frown was irresistible, his lips calling to me even as I formulated words in my mind. Unable to resist his shiny, wet lips, I leaned in to give him a quick kiss. He responded in kind, immediately pulling me close and taking my breath prisoner as his tongue met mine. But then he pulled away just as quickly.

"Nope. No distractions." He held my face gently, looking into my eyes as if I was the only thing in the world. As if I mattered. As if he truly saw me. "You're my mate, and yet I know so little about you. Tell me everything. I want to know you, Zuri."

I sighed and closed my eyes, the warmth his words made me feel at odds with the cold fear caused by his behavior. "You don't play fair."

"Never said I did," he murmured as I huffed and opened my eyes. His nose brushed my cheek, his breath mingling with mine. "Tell me."

One more kiss, irresistible as it was, and then I sighed and settled back against his thighs.

"As a witchling, a child whose magick hasn't bloomed yet, my mom was a student of Sarah Bishop, who was the leader of the Parity Coven for many years. From what I understand, when my mom was pregnant with my sisters and me, she had a vision of her own death. She had no family and no one she trusted with us back home, so she moved north to find Sarah."

"Where was she from, if not Michigan?"

"Florida. There are a lot of independent witches down there—a great mix of magick from different cultures." I leaned back, placing my arms a bit behind to prop myself up. "She came to Sarah for help, and she delivered my sisters and me shortly after she arrived. But she was strong; she held on for three days after our birth before her heart gave out."

Pup reached forward, running his fingers up my cheek. "I'm sorry you never got to meet her."

I looked away as my eyes burned with building tears. "It's okay. Sarah used to tell us stories about her, as both a child and what she knew of her as an adult. My mom was a research junkie, always digging through the library and making notes in the coven's grimoire." I smiled, remembering, voice dropping as I whispered, "I write just like her."

"Do you have pictures?"

I shook my head. "No pictures, but Sarah says Amber looks a lot like her, just with lighter skin."

"Amber's the oldest?"

"Yeah, we're the Weaver triplets. A great gift to the Parity Coven." I rolled my eyes. "Even the death of our mother couldn't calm the coven's excitement. Apparently my mother's ancestors were capable of powerful magick."

"So your witchcraft is hereditary?" His hands ran around my hips and down the sides of my thighs, massaging my ass as they passed.

"Yeah." I groaned as he hit a sore spot in my leg. He reversed his stroke to knead the muscle, which made me sigh and curl my shoulders. "The women of my family and the rest of the Parity families are a powerful bunch. We've done some amazing magick together. Or did, I guess."

My lungs burned under the strain of holding back tears. Speaking of my coven in the past tense was hard, harder than I thought it would be. But I was no longer a part of their group, no matter how much I wanted to be.

Pup's eyes were on my leg, watching his large hands as they worked the muscle kink. "What about the men?"

"There are no male witches."

He glanced at me and raised that eyebrow again. "Really? So what about the men in your coven? What are they like?"

"There are no men in my coven." At his surprised look, I sat up, instantly missing the closeness we'd been enjoying. "There are no boys born to witches, and there are no married or coupled-off witches in our coven. Men are lovely and serve a purpose, but they don't fit in the coven structure."

He didn't move, instead watching me with a look that spoke of wariness. "We don't…fit."

The tone of his voice was enough to set alarm bells off in my head. I wrapped my arms around him and pulled him closer.

"You're different. We're different. I've been gifted a true soul mate, someone who's meant to stand by my side. No one in my coven has found their thread in at least six generations." I kissed his lips, the corner of his mouth, his chin. "You fit with me. We fit together."

His hands slid to my hips, gripping me, pulling me against him as my lips returned to his for a passionate kiss. This was no gentle peck. This was a kiss meant to sear our souls, deep and hot and filled with moans as our bodies rocked with the intensity between us.

I could feel him beneath me, hard and long and wanting. I wanted, too. I wanted him to take me, to ravish me, to push me into a state of bliss. I wanted him to take ownership of my body and my heart, but I was too afraid to tell him. Afraid I'd scare him off with my neediness or shock him with how quickly my feelings for him had deepened.

Instead of words, I used my body. I pressed against him, writhed in his lap, clung to him as he pulled me into a better spot. And when he had me where he wanted, when his dick pressed firm and strong against my clit with a pressure that made me tremble, I sighed a simple "Yes." My whispered plea may not have been loud, but it was enough.

Without pause or preamble, Pup pulled me down and rocked me over his lap. His head tilted to watch as I moaned and gasped with the pressure, with the need. Pulling me tighter, he growled and spun me underneath him, his weight pressing me down. His eyes met mine, so bright with excitement, but his face was again filled with guilt. An expression that brought back my fear.

"Pup? What's wrong? What's on your mind?"

"Jesus, Zuri. I'm sorry…I didn't mean to—"

He stuttered just as a loud knock rattled the door. His forehead landed on my chest with a thump, and he hissed a curse word.

"What is it?"

Pup lifted his head and gave me an apologetic smile. "I have to go to work."

"Work?" I sat up, detangling the two of us. "Now? You really have to go now?"

He huffed a sigh. "Yeah. I do. I'm sorry, I know this is shit timing, but I have to do a job for Rebel. I promise you, I'll be back tomorrow."

My mouth fell open as my stomach bottomed out. "Tomorrow?"

"I know, I'm an ass. I'm sorry." A second knock on the door had Pup growling and yelling. "Give me a goddamned minute, would you?"

Whoever was at the door walked away, their wet footsteps loud on the wood porch. Pup turned back to me, holding my hand and pulling me toward him. Looking incredibly guilty.

"This job is not at all what I want to be doing today, but I came up here for a reason and I need to follow through." He brought his lips to mine in a slow kiss. "I have so much to say to you, so many things to talk about. But I'm out of time."

I sighed into another kiss before pulling away. Even though I didn't feel it, I said what he needed to hear. "It's okay. I'll be fine."

He sat back on his heels. "I have so much to be sorry for—"

I shook my head, fighting to keep my voice even. "No. Don't do that now. Whatever you have to say can wait. The sooner you go, the sooner you can come back."

He dropped his head to my shoulder and sighed. "Yeah, okay." He was up and off the bed before I could reply, before I could stop my heart from burning in my chest at the thought of being left alone in a new place.

"Who knows"—Pup pulled a leather coat on over his sweater and grabbed a matching pair of gloves—"if things go well, I might be back before morning."

I nodded and gave him what had to be a shaky smile. It certainly didn't feel strong. He rushed over to kiss me goodbye, owning my mouth for the briefest of moments.

"I promise, as soon as I get this done, it's nothing but you and me for a while. I have so much to make up to you for. We'll spend a few days together, just the two of us. It'll give us time to talk, and for me to fix my mistakes. We can stay here, go someplace else, whatever. Anything you want."

His smile made a sense of shame roll over me like the tide, building until I felt worse than I did before it began. The man had to work. I'd stormed into his life, into his cabin, taking over and expecting him to capitulate. I could let him go for a day. It was only a matter of hours, really.

"Sure." I took a deep breath and shored up my smile. "That sounds good."

He stopped, his eyes meeting mine. He stared for a long

moment, assessing me, before stepping closer and lifting my chin with his finger.

"I don't want to go, but I promised my Breed brothers I would do this. I swear to you, though, I'll be back as soon as I possibly can, and I'll be missing you the entire time I'm away."

I took a deep breath to hold back the tears threatening to burn a path down my cheeks. "I'll miss you, too."

"Here," Pup said, handing me his phone. "Put your number in."

I typed my information into his phone, sending myself a quick text message so I had his number. Handing him back his phone, I gave him the best smile I could. Pup leaned over me, calm and serious.

"Don't worry." With a final kiss, Pup strode toward the door. "I'll call you when I get there and text you as often as I can, okay?"

I nodded, not wanting my voice to break. But as he grabbed the door handle, as he prepared to exit the little home we now inhabited and walk out into a situation I knew nothing about, I bolted off the bed.

"Wait."

Pup stood and watched me as I rushed to my bag and grabbed a black cloth headband I'd packed in my haste to leave the lighthouse. Facing him, meeting his gaze and holding it, I mentally focused on the energy of the earth around me, particularly the power of the trees and the strength of the wind.

"By knot of one, my spell has begun." I tied a single knot in the headband, twisting the fabric and moving up to do it again.

"By knot of two, it will come true, that my thread shall return anew."

When the second knot was tied, I let the fabric slide through my fingers, twisting one final knot. "By knot of three, so mote it be."

I kept my eyes on Pup's as I closed the space between us and put the knotted fabric in his pocket. "Don't lose it."

He grabbed my elbow when I moved to walk away from him, bending over to give me a deep kiss before whispering against my mouth, "I'm going to love the fuck out of you, little witch. Just you wait and see."

And then he walked out the door.

THIRTEEN

I DIALED ZURI THE second I parked my bobber on Feral Breed property. Seeing her face fall when I told her I had to work had gutted me. For a moment, I'd thought about taking Rebel up on his offer and staying with Zuri instead of dealing with the Kalamazoo den, but I couldn't fail him. He'd given me a job, and I needed to see it through. Then I could deal with groveling for Zuri's forgiveness.

The phone rang twice before a slurring voice that definitely didn't belong to my mate came through the speaker.

"Joe's Morgue. You stab 'em, we bag 'em."

"Hey, uh. Is Zuri there?" I grinned as I heard my mate in the background, yelling at Scarlett for taking her phone.

"What? Are you afraid I'll coerce him with my wit and charm? I'm not trying to steal your man. I was trying to be helpful." Scarlett grunted and there were definite sounds of a scuffle before the giggle of my beautiful mate met my ears.

"Hi, Pup. So you made it down there okay?"

"Yeah, of course." I leaned my bike onto the stand and rested against the seat. "What's going on there? Scarlett causing trouble?"

Zuri huffed. "When isn't she causing trouble? I'm sorry, I was in the bathroom when the phone rang."

"No problem." I had to pause as the roar of a seriously boss engine came from my left. On the far side of the parking lot, a custom chopper rolled to a stop. The gray-haired man riding it quickly dismounted and rushed toward the front door, the telltale limp revealing him as the shifter known as Crash. Leader of the satellite den and the man I needed to talk to. "I only have a minute, babe. But I'm here, I'm safe, and I'm thinking of you."

"I'm thinking of you, too." Her whispered confession made a low rumble start in my chest.

"Good, keep thinking of me until I come home to you." I coughed to hold back my growl, not wanting any of the guys who might come outside to hear me. "I have to get to work, baby. You have fun with your sister and try not to let her lead you astray."

"I heard that, Lassie," Scarlett yelled, her voice carrying through the phone. There was the distinct sound of a fist meeting flesh before Scarlett started whining. "Ow, you bitch. Just for that, I should try to steal him from you. Don't think I can't."

Zuri sighed. "I'm sorry. There're times when I wonder if she was raised by wild animals."

"The only place I'm wild is in the sack, baby!" Scarlett yelled in the background. "C'mon, wolfman. You know you want this."

I laughed. "How drunk are you two?"

Zuri giggled again. "Maybe just a little. Beast brought over some whiskey before he left for his shop."

"He left?" The thought of Beast not being there with my mate while I was working set my world on end for a moment. I knew he had to get the bagger for Rebel, but I figured he'd wait until I was back. Three women in camp and only one shifter there to protect them—I wasn't the biggest fan of those odds. But I reminded myself that the shifter watching over them was Rebel, my leader and friend. He would never let anything happen to my mate.

Zuri hummed her affirmation. "Yeah, he said something about needing to get some bags? I offered him my duffel, but he just laughed."

I shook my head and smiled, still a little uncomfortable about her not being as guarded as I thought she would be, but entertained by her common mistake as well. "Bagger, baby. He went to get Rebel's bagger. It's a kind of motorcycle."

"Oh." She paused, silent, until snorting a chuckle. "No wonder he laughed."

"It's okay. You can teach me about being a witch, and I can teach you about bikes."

"Yes, definitely." She dragged out each syllable, making me wish I were there just to see the way her lips moved. And maybe taste the burn of alcohol on them.

"Okay." I sighed, hating that I had to hang up, not ready to let her go. "You stay close to Rebel. He'll be keeping an eye on you, I'm sure."

She snorted again. "Yeah, Charlotte's here drinking with us and poor Rebel's out on the porch. She told him it was girl time. That big dude left because she told him he couldn't come inside since he has a penis. I don't care that his aura is a mess of colors all the time; he earned points for that."

"Well"—I shrugged even though she couldn't see me—"a wolf wants to make his mate happy."

Her voice dropped, becoming breathy and soft. "You make me happy."

"I'm glad, baby." Anxiety gripped me, making my chest hurt and my skin feel too tight. "I've got to go. I'll text or call as soon as I can."

"Yeah. Okay. And hey, about my sister—"

"Don't worry about it," I said, shaking my head.

"No, I just want you to know you shouldn't take what she says to heart. She's just drunk and mouthy. Scarlett's usually the one chasing guys—"

"Zuri." I grinned as she squeaked, cutting off her own babbling.

"Yeah?"

Growling loud enough for her to hear over the line, I dropped my voice low as I said, "Your sister never had a shot, will never have a shot, and can talk all the crap she wants. I'm yours and yours alone, my mate."

Her gasp came through the phone loud and clear, as did her whispered "Oh. Okay."

I sighed and looked toward the front door of the denhouse, which was definitely not the place I wanted to be. "I have to go."

Zuri sounded just as down as I did when she said, "Right. Work time. Bye, Pup."

"Bye, baby. I'll be missing you." I hung up the phone with a swipe, tucked it into my jacket pocket, and swung my leg over the bike seat. I forced the smile off my face as I approached the door. This was not the time for happy, lovey, newly mated Pup. This was time for Feral Breed Pup. Enforcer of the Detroit den.

The door was locked when I reached it, so I rapped a few times with the back of my knuckles and waited. Seconds later, a voice came over an intercom tucked discreetly beside the door.

"What do you want?"

"I'm here to see Crash."

"No strangers allowed. Get the fuck off our property."

Glaring at the device, I noticed what looked like a camera lens. I turned just enough for whoever was playing the part of the Wizard of Oz to see the cut on my back. Even without the wolf insignia, I knew the Feral Breed rocker on the top would be enough to get me inside.

"Pretty sure this is all our property, man. Now let me in—Rebel sent me."

There was a few seconds pause before the locks unlatched and a young shifter in a black T-shirt pulled the door open.

"Crash will be out in a few." The kid stepped back so I could enter. What met me was pretty much what I'd expected. Shifters sat around the room, watching TV or playing cards, bottles of beer littering the tables, and a hazy cloud of smoke floating through the air.

Four huge flat-screen televisions were mounted over the bar, each showing a different football game in progress. Money exchanged hands on every play as bets were won and lost, and shifters cheered or groaned over the performance of their preferred team. Pretty much a typical Sunday in a denhouse.

But then I saw the five smaller TVs behind the bar. Each had a view of outside the building, focusing on the door, the parking lot, the gated driveway, and even the road leading in.

"Is that live feed?"

The kid I'd asked looked nervous, but another denmate sitting at the bar spoke up.

"Gotta keep our team safe."

I stared at the screens, realizing how many other shifters kept taking glances at them as my blood began to chill in my veins. "Safe from what?"

A new voice chimed in. "From things that go bump in the night."

I turned as Crash, the leader Rebel assigned to run the Kalamazoo branch, strode into the room. Big, broad, and inked from his fingertips to his jawline, the man exuded a vibe that had made me quake in my boots the first time I'd met him. But no longer. Crash was a lot of things, but a threat to me wasn't one of them.

"Aren't we technically the things that go bump in the night?" I reached out to grasp his hand as he offered it, giving it a single hearty shake before slapping him on the opposite shoulder. "It's good to see you, though I wish it were under better circumstances."

He huffed and growled. "Circumstances couldn't really get much worse. Come on back. We can chill in my office."

I followed him down a hall, the noise of the shifters in the main bar disappearing as we walked deeper into the labyrinth of old office spaces at the back of the building. When we reached the closed door to his office, he stopped long enough to tap four times, pause, then tap twice more before opening it. He stepped in quickly, the speed at which he moved surprising me. Before I could comment, I walked into the room and immediately froze.

The young shifter who'd opened the front door for me sat on a couch, a rifle resting across the arm. Pointed right at me.

The growl that rolled through my chest was as loud as any I'd ever released. "What the hell is going on here?"

Crash settled into a seat behind the desk and leaned back. "What the hell is going on in Detroit?"

I glanced at him but quickly turned back to the young shifter with the weapon. "I have no idea what you're talking about."

Crash slammed his fist on the desktop. "We've been calling for over a week trying to rouse some help to hunt down whoever ganked Spook, but no one's calling us back. And now you show up all by yourself. Where is everyone?"

"It ain't like I've got them LoJacked. Who you looking for?"

"Rebel, Magnus, Gates...we've tried them all. No one's answering their damn phones."

"Rebel and Gates are newly mated, they've been taking a break. And Magnus is out at the Fields getting his knee worked on. Our last mission for Blaze put him out of commission."

Crash glared at me for a moment before sighing and running a hand over his face. "Fuck me. I knew I should have sent Goober to the D to deliver the message in person."

"What message? And hey, do you mind?" I turned a palm up at the kid with the gun. Crash rolled his eyes.

"Put it away, Spank. I've got this covered."

The kid slid the gun under the couch and quickly left the room, leaving me wondering if I should be glad he was so good at listening to Crash's orders or scared of what he could be doing out in the main room.

"Jesus, way to welcome a guy, Crash." I dropped onto the couch Spank had vacated. "What the hell is going on around here?"

"What the fuck are you doing here if you don't know what the problem is?"

I shrugged. "I'm here because of the missing money."

Crash stared at me for a long moment before howling with laughter. "That's rich. Leave it to Rebel to be more concerned about his precious Draught money than his Breed brothers."

I snarled and swung my arm, crashing my fist into the desktop and cracking the wood. Crash stopped laughing and stared at me.

"I don't know what's going on or why no one's called you back, but don't disrespect our president that way."

Crash rose to his feet, a mountain of a man gliding up to his full, almost seven foot height. "When he acts like a president, I'll respect him like one."

I growled again as I stood, ready to battle the ass with the attitude, but a whimper from the other side of the desk stopped me. I turned, shame building as I realize a young boy was curled into the space between Crash's desk and the wall, shaking as if terrified.

"Oh, hey. I didn't mean—"

Crash shook his head and held up his hand. "He's okay. He's just not used to seeing the violent side of shifters." He pulled the boy from his hiding spot and wrapped an arm around him, even though the little one barely came up to his hip. "He's my son, but he's been raised in the human world."

I glanced between them, confusion heavy in my mind. "I wasn't aware you were mated."

With a deep breath, Crash raised his chin, almost in challenge. "I'm not, but I claimed his mother as mine nearly ten years ago. We've got four kids together. Joshua here is my oldest." He grinned in that quintessential proud papa way. "He's the only shifter in the bunch."

Crash held my gaze as understanding washed over me. He'd never mated, but grown tired of being alone as some shifters did. By claiming a human woman as his, he'd given her the protection of the shifters who respected Crash, but none of the benefits. She'd die long before he did, as would any children they had who didn't carry the shifter gene. It wasn't the most common choice, but claiming a human happened enough not to shock me. What did was that his son was a shifter but being raised in the human world.

The fact that Rebel had never mentioned Crash's family made me wonder if he even knew about them.

I dropped to one knee so as to look the young man in the face. "It's nice to meet you, Joshua. My name's Pup, and I'm sorry I scared you."

The kid sniffed and pressed harder against Crash's leg. "It's okay."

"Joshua here has become obsessed with what his daddy does for a living." Crash smiled down at his son. "He's a brave young man; will make a good addition to the Breed when he comes into his own."

"I bet." I rose to my full height, thoughts of Zuri and kids and what would happen when the Breed knew I'd mated swirling in my mind. "So Spook's off the grid, is that right?"

Crash sighed and settled into his chair as Joshua stared at me from his father's side.

"Yeah, and it's got me worried." Crash tapped one finger on the desktop. "Spook's not a thief, no matter what anyone says. The guy's as solid as they come. But then he stops showing up, and there's a big chunk of change missing that he's responsible for."

"You think he bogarted the money and ran?"

Crash shook his head. "Not in a million years. First, it's not his way. Guy's been getting a little squirrely in his old age but no worse than any other non-mated centenarian shifter. And second, it's not enough money to really get that far, you know? If he was going to go down in those kinds of flames, you'd think he'd steal a full month's take or something. This was piddly when you think about spending the rest of your life on the run. No, I don't think he took it."

"And no one's seen or heard from him?"

"Nope. Not a peep. I drove out to his house last week to see what I could find, but the place was empty with no sign he'd been there."

I rubbed my thumb down my cheek, letting my mind wander. If Spook didn't take the cash, it had to be someone around him. There really was no other excuse for the money and the shifter to go missing at the same time. But I didn't know enough about Spook to know who might be the perpetrator.

"Mind if I head over to his place? I'd like to take a look around."

Crash shrugged. "Sure. I'll even come with you. Gotta

make sure you don't get lost." He reached for the phone sitting on his desk and pressed a few numbers. "Send Spank back."

I smirked as we waited for the young shifter. "Spank?"

Crash chuckled. "Those TVs aren't just for football, and the kid's young. A few too many extra-long visits to the john, and the name was born."

I chuckled as the kid in question walked in.

"Yeah, boss?"

Crash rose to his feet once more. "Keep an eye on Joshua for me. Pup and I have a little errand to run."

"Sure thing." The kid walked behind the desk and reached out a hand to the younger boy. Crash and I walked out of the office together, heading toward the noise of the main room.

"No cut for Spank?" I asked.

Crash shook his head. "He's just a hanger-on for now. He'll earn his Pup status when he grows up a bit; then we'll really see what he's made of."

I snorted. "Let's hope he earns a better road name than Spank."

"Truth. No one will ever want to shake his hand."

Ten minutes later, the two of us dismounted our bikes and looked over the little, yellow house that had been home to Spook until a few weeks ago.

"Looks…cozy." I shrugged as Crash laughed. "What? It looks like a home."

"It should. Spook's lived here for close to twenty years."

We walked up the pathway to the front porch. I tried looking in the front window, but there was some kind of fabric hanging in the way and blocking my view. When I turned back to the door, Crash was picking a key up from under the front mat.

"Really?" I scoffed.

Crash shrugged. "The guy didn't worry. There ain't much

that can take out an old shifter like Spook when he's protecting his den."

I followed Crash inside when he opened the door. The interior looked just as homey and comfortable as the exterior, though something about the house didn't feel right. A smell, a stack of newspapers near the couch, an empty beer can on the side table. I walked over to the newspapers, running my finger across the front page of the top one.

"Three days ago." I glanced over my shoulder at Crash. "You sure he's not been around?"

"Positive." Crash's nostrils flared as he sniffed and looked around the room. "What the fuck is that smell?"

It was my turn to shrug. "No clue. You check out the whole house last time?"

"Nah, just this room and the kitchen. I didn't want to get too far into his business. Besides, it's not like the place looked as if it'd been busted into."

"Yeah, well, it's Breed business now. Let's check it all." I led the way through the house, finding nothing of interest in the kitchen, bathroom, or dining room. Crash walked into the bedroom as I peeked in the small bathroom, noting the still-damp towel on the bar and the toothbrush in the holder.

"Pup, I think you'd better come look at this."

I walked across the hallway and into the bedroom. "There's definitely been someone—"

The words died on my tongue as I looked past Crash to the far wall of the room. Pictures. From floor to ceiling, every inch was covered in pictures. Color and black and white, close-ups and landscape style shots of Lake Michigan, the dunes, the trees, an old lighthouse…

"That looks like Lake Parity." Crash pointed to the brick building, tower spearing the sky above. "Why would he be fixated on that old lighthouse?"

My heart nearly stopped as his words registered. I scanned the pictures again, looking for signs that he was wrong, hoping against hope that I wouldn't find a picture of—

"Scarlett."

Crash looked at me as if I had three heads. "Huh?"

I pointed to a black and white picture taped to the wall at my hip level. "Her name's Scarlett."

"You know her?" He dropped down to get a better look.

I nodded, unable to form words as my eyes scanned the pictures for more signs of people. The wall was covered, mostly in shots of the lakes, trees, and a lighthouse.

"They keep going." Crash fingered a picture bent around the closet trim, disappearing behind the door itself. With my heart in my throat and a cold sweat forming all over my body, I gripped the knob and pulled open the closet door.

"Motherfucker." My words came out on a whisper, harsh but quiet.

"Gods be gracious." Crash stood beside me, staring into what could only be described as a shrine.

Most of the pictures covering every square inch of the walls, floor, and ceiling were of a young woman I didn't recognize, though something about her seemed familiar. The curve of her jaw, the golden skin and dark hair, the dimple that only showed when she truly grinned.

But Spook hadn't stopped at pictures. Scraps of fabric, bowls of what looked like soil, a glove, a candy wrapper, a chewed piece of gum, a few strands of dark hair. They covered a small table in the center of the space, a sign hanging from the front of it. One word painted in black.

MINE

"You okay, Pup?"

Crash's words barely sank through the fear and fury that swamped me as I focused on a particular picture. This one with three young women together. All with golden skin and dark hair. Red lips. Big smiles on their faces.

Scarlett, Zuri, and the woman of Spook's obsession. The woman I had to assume was the third Weaver sister, Amber.

Without warning or explanation, I ran for my bike as I dialed Zuri's number.

"Pick up, pick up, pick up."

When her sweet voice came over the line, I felt a moment of relief before rage swelled in my gut.

"You've reached Azurine Weaver. Leave me a message and I'll call you back."

"Zuri. I need you to stay with Rebel. No matter what happens, stay with Rebel. I'm on my way."

Crash came running up beside me as I mounted my bobber. "What the fuck, Pup?"

I snarled, fury and fear mixing into a toxic combination beneath my skin. "Spook's a dead man."

"What?"

I met his confused gaze as I yanked on my gloves. "The three girls in those pictures are witches, triplet sisters of a coven on Parity Lake. Spook must have become obsessed with the one he made his stalker-shrine for, Amber. He's crossed into a feral shifter at best and a man-eater at worst. Either way, he's a danger to himself, the secret, and to those girls."

"While I get the need to control him if he's gone man-eater, why should we give a shit about a group of fucking witches?"

I looked him right in the eye, rage burning inside me and making it hard to utter the words I needed him to hear. The explanation he needed to be able understand the level of fucked up this was.

"One of the girls in the pictures, one of the witches, is named Azurine. She's my mate."

Crash's jaw dropped as he stared at me. But then he growled.

"What the fuck are you doing here if you've got a mate? Mated wolves don't ride!"

His words stung, hitting home with their truth in more ways than I would've expected. Pushing down my guilt, I nodded, my gut locked tight as terror raced through my veins. "Call Beast and Rebel. Keep calling them until you reach one of them. Let them know I'm coming back and that the Weaver girls are in danger. All three of them."

FOURTEEN

"YOU'RE A JERK." SCARLETT huffed and rubbed her arm where I'd punched her.

"Well, you're an idiot for talking that way." I dropped my phone on the table.

"You two crack me up." Charlotte grinned from where she lay sprawled on the floor, whiskey bottle in hand. "I'm so glad we got to have a girls' day."

"Yeah, though we can't really get into any good details with your guard dog out there." Scarlett lifted her chin toward the front door. Rebel's growl could be heard from the porch, making the three of us giggle.

Charlotte waved her hands to get our attention then gave us a huge wink. "Eh, there's not that many details to begin with. I'm always working, and my brother's home, and Rebel, well, I mean, he is over four hundred years old."

"Wait, you suck four-hundred-year-old dick?" Scarlett looked mortified. Poor Charlotte started to laugh, but then stopped, looking surprised.

"Well, shit, I guess I do." Charlotte stood and wobbled toward the door. "I think you should tell me where the hell that thing's been for the last four hundred years. I don't know that I want it near me."

"Keep it up, Cherry." Rebel yelled through the closed door. "If I remember correctly, you definitely wanted this four-hundred-year-old dick near you last night. All six times."

Scarlett's mouth dropped open as she mouthed *Six?* at a beaming, nodding Charlotte.

"Damn," Scarlett exclaimed. "Where can I find me a wolf?"

"Stay away from mine," Charlotte and I spoke in unison, laughing as soon as we finished.

"Brats. Both of you." Scarlett rolled onto her back and lifted her legs in the air, pointing her toes at the ceiling. "Though there is that succulent Beast hanging around. I could go for a little beard burn on my thighs, if you know what I mean."

Charlotte looked at me, her eyes unfocused and her movements uncoordinated. "I'm not sure I know what you mean. How do you get it on your thighs?"

Scarlett's grin turned wicked. "Well, when a man has a beard, and he goes down to the holy land—"

Rebel threw open the door, a low rumble vibrating in his chest as he homed in on Charlotte. "I hate to break up the party—"

"No, you don't," the three of us said in unison.

"You're right. I don't."

"So tell me, Rebel," Scarlett started, looking blearily at the handsome shifter. "How is it you can give this woman six— *six!*—orgasms in one night, but she's never had beard burn on her thighs? Are you anti-face-riding, or do you shave too much?"

"Jesus." Rebel looked at the ceiling as Charlotte and I laughed. "You girls are trouble."

"Totally." I walked over to my bag, looking for a pair of socks as the floors were a bit cold in the cabin. Pup's duffel sat unzipped next to mine. A ratty sweatshirt peeked out from inside, gray and soft-looking from wear. I shrugged a shoulder and pulled it out of the bag. I wanted to have his scent on me, wanted him to fill my senses as if he were here. This yearning for another person was new for me, and I had no idea how to handle it.

"Oh yeah, do that," Charlotte said, waving the bottle in my direction. "He'll love that."

"You don't think he'll mind?"

She laughed, a loud, booming sound that made me smile. "Fuck no, he won't mind. We'll all be lucky if he gives us time to get out of the cabin once he see you in it."

My cheeks heated as I thought of Pup so turned on by me wearing his clothes that he couldn't wait to be alone. How his hands would slide under the fabric. How he'd pull at it as he owned my mouth. The way his fingers—

"Quit daydreaming and put it on." Scarlett huffed and turned over while Charlotte laughed again.

"Are you sure?" I asked. This time it was Rebel who laughed.

"Zuri, we're wolves. Any sign of our claim on our mate is…a positive thing."

"Positive?" Charlotte leaned toward me. "I bought this shirt that had Rebel printed in bright letters across the girls, and you'd have thought I'd painted my breasts—"

"Okay, that's enough." Rebel picked Charlotte up and carried her out the door, whispering, "You brought that shirt, didn't you?"

Cheeks burning, I hurried into the bathroom and stripped out of my skirt and sweater, leaving me in a tank top and panties. I pulled the sweatshirt over my head and laughed as it swallowed me from shoulders to knees. It took three rolls of each sleeve to keep the cuffs above my fingers, but it was warm and smelled like Pup. I strolled back into the bedroom and pulled a pair of knee socks out of my bag to keep my legs warm.

Scarlett snored softly from where she'd passed out on the bed. I shook my head and picked up the cabin to kill time. Dirty clothes, a few slips of paper, a magazine—all small things that cluttered the tiny space. If I was going to live here with Pup for a while, I'd have to figure out how to earn my rent. I didn't have a job outside the coven, had never needed one since I ran the web store of the pagan supply company Sarah had started. Once Pup and I decided where to live, I'd have to find work. Definitely a daunting thought.

My stomach rolled as I imagined moving away. Would Scarlett go with us? Or would she choose to go back to the coven? And Amber—the idea of not having Amber around to temper our personalities was painful. She was the mature one, the little momma, always trying to keep us in line. Scarlett was the crazy one, in more trouble than out of it. I was neither as controlling as Amber nor as wild as Scarlett, but I always knew I had a place with my sisters.

I sighed and gripped the receipt for the pizzas Pup and I had shared as an early lunch, my heart hurting and a melancholy settling over me like a summer storm—sudden and overpowering. I was going to lose parts of my family no matter what decision I made. Pup was wonderful and I could see a life with him, but my sisters were my past. They were my present and supposed to be a big part of my future. They were my blood. We weren't *us* without the three sides being together.

Depressed and missing Pup madly, I laid down beside Scarlett, curling into her side. The whiskey had made me sad and sleepy, a combination too seductive to resist.

MINUTES OR HOURS LATER, a knock startled me awake. I uncurled myself from around a still-sleeping Scarlett and walked to the door. What met me when I opened it nearly took my breath away.

"I think we need to talk." Amber walked in as if invited, wrinkling her nose as she looked around.

"Sure thing, sis. Come right in." I closed the door behind her, my face burning and back straight. If she dared to say something about this homey little cabin—

"Day drinking? Is that how far you two have fallen?" She waved at a still sleeping Scarlett.

"What do you want, Amber? I know you're not here to talk about alcohol."

She turned, a frown on her face. "How could you do it, Zuri? How could you turn your back on the coven? I thought we were a family?"

I stood immobile, staring at her as the tangled web of her words slowly worked its way up through the darkness inside of me.

"How could I? You shunned me. And when that wasn't good enough, you banished me."

"Because you betrayed us!" Amber stepped closer, pointing a finger in my face. "You knew there were wolves in the woods, but you didn't tell us. You said nothing when you called, just that you were safe and would be home later. But you didn't come home. We had to come get you after we found wolf tracks by the house. If we would've known they were from yours, we wouldn't have worried so much or risked coming into a camp full of those animals. You put your entire coven in danger so you could make out with a man you'd only just met."

"What are you talking about? Pup's never been to the lighthouse."

Amber paused, her brow furrowing for a moment before she huffed. "Then the tracks were left by one of his friends; how else do you explain them?"

"Uh, I don't know. Maybe a wolf came to visit?"

"Yeah, right. As if there just happen to be more wolves in these woods than the ones you're fucking around with."

"Amber, when Scarlett and I found the camp, all three of the guys who shift into wolves were here. I would think they would've told me if they'd been sneaking around the lighthouse."

Amber raised her eyebrows, picking at the one thing I'd said that hung like a loose thread. "Maybe they're not being as honest with you as you think they are."

I shrugged, her words making me uncomfortable. "The Fates called me here, to this campground, and to Pup. I trust him."

"And what about us?" Her voice lowered, her face showing her betrayal. "You leave your coven behind because you believe the Fates planned for you to be the broodmare for some wild dog?"

I struck without thinking, knocking her off her feet with my open hand. "Take it back."

The floor beneath my feet rumbled as she held her cheek with one hand, flicking her fingers with the other. "No. You're being a selfish brat. You turned your back on your family."

"You banished me!" The cabin shook with the force of our magicks fighting against one another. Water and air joined into a storm that rumbled through the small space. The air turned humid as it blew around the room, an indoor tornado building, ready to rip the ceiling down.

"You left me to deal with everything!" Amber's wind increased in strength, making my hair whip around my head and slash across my face. "Sarah's dying, the coven's panic. You and Scarlett disappeared into the woods without telling me anything, and you expect me to clean up the mess you left behind. Why can't you just grow up and be responsible?"

A crash sounded as Amber pushed a wave of energy my

way, knocking over a chair instead. Before I could strike back, Rebel rushed through the door, grabbing Amber from behind and holding her off the floor.

"What the hell is going on in here?"

Amber struggled against his hold to no avail. The winds calmed as he held her, leaving us all damp from the water now condensing on the window and walls.

"Just sisters being sisters," Scarlett said as she stood from the bed. "That one you've got in a choke hold is the oldest Weaver triplet."

"Want me to let her go?"

Scarlett tilted her head, considering it. "No."

"Yes." I frowned at Scarlett. "Let her go; she won't hurt us on purpose."

Amber coughed as Rebel let her down. "Touch me again, you beast, and I'll kill you where you stand."

"Your sister's not invited to girls' day, ever." Charlotte stood in the doorway, glaring at Amber. "Threaten my mate again, and I'll throw a bucket of water on you."

"This isn't some cheesy movie. We don't melt."

"Stop." I held my hands up, my head aching and my heart tired of being battered. "Amber, why did you come here? We know it wasn't some goodwill gesture."

Amber glared, breathing hard as she looked from me to Scarlett. "Sarah wants to see you both. She sent me to bring you home."

Fury. Absolute and fiery hot, fury exploded within me. Holding it back as best I could, I walked up to my sister, nearly brushing my nose against hers. "You banished me from the coven, which means I can no longer live at the lighthouse. I am home."

Her face fell, her eyes growing shiny with what looked like tears. But that didn't last. She took a deep breath before her face hardened into a mask of anger. "Yeah, well…she still wants to see you."

"Fine." I grabbed a pair of leggings out of my bag and pulled them up my legs. "I'll go see Sarah. But then that's it. If you and the coven can't accept Pup in my life, then we have nothing left to say."

FIFTEEN

I ROARED INTO CAMP, tires slipping on the semi-frozen ground as I raced toward my cabin. Zuri hadn't called me or answered the handful of times I'd risked dialing while riding. Neither had Rebel, who should have been watching over her. The lack of communication didn't help the panic bubbling within me.

Not willing to waste a single second, I laid my bike down in front of the cabin, hopping off as it skidded. Two slips and I was racing up the stairs.

"Zuri!" I threw open the door and ran inside. "Fuck."

The cabin sat empty. A near-empty whiskey bottle lay on the bed. Zuri's bag was open, resting on the floor beside mine. Yet she wasn't there. Her scent permeated the cabin, fading a bit from her full, in-person strength. If I had to guess, I'd say she'd left within the last hour or so. Which meant she was trackable.

I grabbed my phone and called her for what had to be the tenth time. Her phone lit up from where it lay on the table, making me roar in frustration. I was about to shift, to sniff her out and follow her trail, when I heard the rumble of a big vehicle coming closer. Running outside, I bolted for the entrance road, praying that she was in the truck. That she was safe and coming back to me. That I was overreacting.

But it was only Beast's face through the windshield when the truck turned off the main road.

He slammed the brakes and threw the truck in park when he saw me running toward him. Opening the door, he jumped down and immediately ran in my direction. "What's wrong?"

I panted as my mind spun, unable to stop on a single thought. "Spook. Zuri. Not here."

Beast grabbed my shoulders and leaned in, bringing his face eye level with mine. "Is she in trouble?"

I nodded, still unable to catch my breath.

"Okay." He pulled his coat off and tossed it on the hood of his truck. "Shift, we'll track her from here."

I swallowed and moved to turn, but Beast held me still. "Calm, boy. You'll end up a twisted mess of bones and flesh if you try to shift in this state."

Holding eye contact, I took three deep breaths. The effect was calming, though not nearly as much as normal. Not even his maker mojo could completely take away the anxiety rolling through me. Only Zuri, safe, and back in my arms.

"Spook's after the sister, Amber," I said breathlessly once I could focus on my words. "But he had pictures of all three."

"Okay." Beast patted my shoulders and took a step back. "We'll find them. I want you to shift and lead the way. Your bond will tell you where your mate is even faster than my nose."

I nodded and breathed deep, searching for the slight tug on the thread joining me to Zuri. In my panic, I'd forgotten how the two of us were joined; thank God Beast hadn't. I carried her essence in my blood; I could track her by feel as well as scent. And as long as I felt that pull, I knew she was alive.

Reaching in my pocket, I pulled out the knotted stretchy thing Zuri had given me. I wrapped it around my wrist, hoping it would make it through a shift. With little more than a prayer for Zuri's safety, I shifted to my wolf form. My discarded clothing flew behind me as I untangled myself from their hold. The second my paws hit dirt, I ran full bore in the direction my bond told me to go. Beast followed at my shoulder—a black-as-pitch shadow with a vicious scar on one side of his face—racing into the woods without question or fear.

We'd find her.

We had to.

Azurine

"YOU COULD SLOW DOWN, you know." I stumbled over a tree root, cursing as I almost fell.

"Or you could try to keep up." Amber practically glided down the trail, head up and anger clouding her aura. "Some of us have responsibilities, you know."

"Ladies." Rebel followed us, holding on to Charlotte's hand to keep her from falling. Seeing them, the way he led her around puddles and rough spots, made me miss Pup. I cursed myself for the tenth time since we left the cabin for not grabbing my phone on the way out the door.

"I have responsibilities." I swung wide around a large puddle, slipping in the soft mud.

Amber glanced my way, smirking when she saw how my shoes were covered in muck. "Right, you have them; you just have no clue how to honor them. You prefer to leave everything for other people to handle so you can run off with your latest toy."

"Ladies." Rebel's voice was darker, his frustration showing. Something Amber must have noticed as well.

"You know, you can shut it anytime now, wolf." Amber looked over her shoulder, glaring at the shifter as he directed Charlotte over a fallen branch. "And hey, how about you tell whichever of your friends has been hanging around outside the lighthouse to stay away. I don't need your kind of protection."

Rebel frowned, looking confused. "What are you talking about?"

"The footprints, the wolf sightings, the howls." Amber shook her head and scoffed as Rebel just stared back at her, silent. "What, are you going to try and deny it was one of your guys? Like I'm supposed to believe there's another group of wolves in the woods."

"Maybe not group," Rebel said, his voice deepening into a slight growl. Charlotte looked up at him, worry clear in her expression. "It wasn't us."

She huffed. "By the Goddess, now Zuri's attracting a whole pack to us."

"Amber." Rebel moved a step closer, reaching for her as if to keep her from running. But then he stopped and turned… slowly.

"What?" My sister didn't look at him, just continued walking along the trail on the way to the lighthouse.

"Amber, I think you should—"

"Amber."

We all spun at the unfamiliar voice coming from behind us. A man stood on the trail, looking at Amber with an expression of joy unlike any I'd seen before. He was tall and muscular, wearing a leather jacket and jeans much like Rebel. But unlike Rebel, this man appeared almost sickly, with his pale skin, eyes of an indeterminate watery color, and an overall air of neglect. He seemed…disturbed, dirty, and wrong.

"Spook?" Rebel took a step toward the man as he questioned him. "What are you doing out here?"

Spook's smile fell as he tried to focus on Rebel, but his eyes kept returning to Amber. Small movements, tics almost, as if he couldn't stop himself from watching her. "Crash sent me.

Said there was some trouble up this way and y'all needed help."

Rebel hummed and stepped toward the man. He moved slowly, deliberately, like an animal stalking prey. As he edged along the path, he directed Charlotte back to where I stood behind him. Placing himself solidly between us and the threat on the trail. Scarlett stepped closer as well, and Amber walked over to join us.

"Did you talk to Pup?" Rebel's voice came out calm, showing no sign of the wariness I knew he had to be feeling. "I sent him down to Kalamazoo to see you."

The man seemed nervous, eyes bouncing from Rebel to Amber to the woods at my left and back to Rebel. "Yeah. Sure did. He'll be back in a few hours. Cybil was down at the den today, so Pup was a little preoccupied. That's why Crash sent me. You know how those young bucks get around the shewolves."

My heart stopped for a beat as my mind flashed to the guilt on Pup's face before he left. But there was no way he'd do something that would hurt me like spending time with another woman, wolf or no.

I'm yours and yours alone, my mate.

I trusted him, implicitly.

Rebel chuckled, the sound completely wrong. "There's no way that's what happened, man. Pup's found his mate."

Spook looked surprised for a moment before dropping his gaze to the ground. "Sure, yeah. Maybe I misunderstood. But Crash did tell me to come here."

"Of course he did; we were looking for help." Rebel took another step forward, his shoulders tight and his body angled as if on defense. "What'd Crash say to do? Is there a plan?"

Spook suddenly looked excited, eyes blinking multiple times as he looked us over.

"Of course...of course there's a plan. I'm supposed to take the girls back to the lighthouse. The old one's sick; she needs them home." He caught me in his gaze, his glare blistering even from where he stood. "Scar and Zuri shouldn't have left the way they did. It was too much for Amber to handle on her own."

A chill of dread went up my spine, something so wrong about the fact that this stranger knew who I was. That he knew my nickname. That he knew what the three of us had been doing. Yet I'd never seen him before.

"Yeah, it's been a rough couple of days," Rebel said as he glanced over his shoulder at us. He caught my eye, looking meaningfully at Charlotte before coming back to me. It was subtle and fast, but I understood what he meant. Get his mate out of the way. Keep her safe. Because he was about to do something dangerous.

"Well, Spook," Rebel said, turning to face the shifter. "I was just taking the girls to the lighthouse myself, so I don't think you're going to be needed."

"What? No."

"Sorry, man. But I've got this covered. I think you should be on your way back to the denhouse."

As Spook began to shake and growl, I crept closer to Charlotte, nudging her toward a giant tree just off the path. It was big enough to hide her behind, should we need to. As we moved, Rebel was also making minor adjustments. Unzipping his coat, cracking his neck, moving his feet to keep himself between Spook and us.

"I want to take them." Spook looked nervous at that point, twitching and shaking and staring at Amber, who was cowering with Scarlett on the other side of Charlotte.

Rebel shook his head and put his hands on his hips. "That's not going to happen, man."

"Rebel, I need them." Spook stopped, took a deep breath, and then looked our way. "Her. I need her, been waiting for her. Just the one. Give me Amber."

Rebel snarled as he edged closer to Spook. "That's not happening either."

Spook's face went slack as he stared at my sister. No emotion, no movement. Just a flat, dread-inducing blankness that made him ten times more frightening than he'd been as he twitched and argued.

Then he shrugged.

"Then I'll have to kill you all."

Spook shifted into wolf form, clothing falling to the ground as light gray fur appeared where there had been only skin. Rebel shifted just as fast, already running toward the man as his jeans fell to the ground. Similarly colored, too difficult to tell apart, they streaked in a blur of gray and white fur to the center of the path. The two met in a collision of fur and teeth, snarling in a way that made the hair on the back of my neck stand on end. Two predators, fighting to the death only a few yards away.

Charlotte yelped when I pushed her against the tree. I faced out, blocking her, keeping her tucked behind me. Scarlett stood at my left, Amber at my right, the three of us using the tree to completely box poor Charlotte in.

"I've got this." Scarlett's fingers glowed as she lifted her hand.

"No." I grabbed her wrist, keeping my eyes on the two wolves fighting. "You could hurt Rebel."

We watched the fighting, feeling helpless. I could have called the rain or pulled the water from their skin, but whatever I did to Spook would probably affect Rebel. There was no way to isolate them. No way for my magick to focus on the correct wolf when I wasn't sure who was who.

"We should run," Amber said, her voice a little shaky.

"Absolutely not." I gripped her elbow and pulled her closer as the growling increased. "We have to keep Charlotte safe for Rebel. Besides, if we run, Spook will chase us. He's a wolf, remember? He's got instincts and shit."

"But what about—"

Her question was cut off as one of the wolves squealed in pain. The two were so close in color, so fast as they jumped and clawed, it was nearly impossible to tell who was who. The only obvious difference was that one was suddenly bleeding from a wound in its throat.

"Rebel!" Charlotte cried as she tried to push past us.

"No." I turned and plastered my body against hers. "You have to stay here; you'll distract him too much if he thinks you're in danger."

She peered at me, tears in her eyes and fear plain on her face. "I don't want to lose him."

"I know. But we can't—"

"Fuck, there's more of them," Amber yelled. I spun, my mouth falling open as Pup in his wolf form raced into the field. Tall, strong, and dark enough to easily distinguish from Rebel and Spook, he demanded attention. It was something in the way he ran, the way his body moved, how he focused so completely on the fighting wolves. He was an impressive man, but in his animal form, he was positively captivating.

Pup ran straight for the other two wolves with a larger black wolf racing alongside him—Beast. Growling and snarling, Pup leapt over the last few feet between him and Spook. He slammed into the injured wolf, knocking him to the ground and biting his neck with a viciousness that made my stomach turn. Charlotte screamed as the gray wolf fell, landing in a heap of fur and blood with Pup standing over him.

"Abraham."

I shook my head, about to tell her about Pup and how there was no way he'd have attacked Rebel, until...

Out of the corner of my eye, I caught a small motion. A tiny flicker that made my stomach plummet as time slowed almost to the point of standing still. The next second dragged, giving me plenty of time to realize that Amber thought Pup was our enemy. She'd seen him kill a gray wolf; indistinguishable from the one supposed to be protecting us. She thought she'd seen Pup kill Rebel, and she was going to use her magick to stop him. Arms out, fingers extended, reaching toward where my mate stood. And even though I couldn't hear the words she chanted, I knew the spell she'd choose. Knew exactly what was about to happen with a surety that reeked of divination.

Terror built within me as her fingers curled, her hands cupping. I yelled, the sound hindered and distorted in the slower reality, taking far too long to travel from my mouth to Amber's ears. Too slow to help my Pup, to give him a heads up. Far too slow.

And as her thumb met her fingertips and the magick exploded out of her, time sped back to normal.

My scream shattered the near-silence around me, but it was too late. The spell hit Pup with enough force to knock him over. His wolf lay on his side, feet paddling and claws extended as his tongue lolled. He gasped—once, twice, fighting to breathe, air-starved and suffering—before his body morphed from fur to skin, wolf to human.

Naked and still gasping for air, he met my eyes, his mouth open as he tried to inhale. But he couldn't, not with the spell Amber used. She'd practiced it defensively for years, perfected it when the other air witches had failed. It was a magickal depressurization, sucking the air from his lungs and collapsing them in the process. The rapid evacuation of air led to a suction power within the lungs, making it impossible to reinflate by the one attacked. Effective, fast, and deadly, it was the only spell I'd never seen her be able to reverse.

SIXTEEN

NOSES TO THE GROUND, we followed the scents left by the girls. And Rebel. His presence had made me feel calmer about Zuri being in the woods. But as we hurried down the trail, snarls reached our ears. Hearing the vicious sound of a wolf battle stole that calm. I pushed myself harder, faster, desperate to get to Zuri. I needed to find her, to protect her.

Turning a final bend, we came upon a scene that made my hackles rise. Rebel, in wolf form, fighting a second gray wolf. One I didn't recognize except by scent. Spook: the missing Breed member, thief, and collector of pictures of my mate and her sisters.

Rebel had the upper hand in the fight, attacking the smaller wolf aggressively while Spook ducked and tried to avoid our leader's jaws. Zuri and her sisters stood farther down the path, the three Weaver sisters forming a protective arc in front of a terrified looking Charlotte, Relief flooded me as I saw my mate unharmed.

Knowing my mate was safe, I rushed toward the fighting wolves just as Rebel's teeth sliced through part of Spook's throat. It wasn't a death bite, but it was enough to stun and confuse the wolf. His inattention was my chance, my opportunity, and I took it. Leaping, I landed with my teeth in his neck and twisted, ripping out his throat with a single move. Blood poured from the wound, painting me in his death, but I didn't care. Knowing I'd eliminated a threat to my mate and her family made me puff up with pride.

But just as fast, fear gripped my heart and my chest tightened to the point of pain. I whimpered as the pressure increased, making it impossible to breathe. Dizzy and off-balance, I gasped and fell to the ground. Black spots edged into my vision, growing larger with every second that passed without air reaching my lungs.

Struggling to stay conscious, I shifted to my human form, still unable to breathe. There was nothing I could do. Nothing that would relieve the pressure on my chest. As the spots grew to nearly cover my field of vision, I looked over to my Zuri. The pain and fear on her face gutted me. I tried to crawl to her but I fell to the dirt. Chest tight. No room. Not enough energy to gasp.

As I mentally fell into a pool of light, filled with water the same color as Zuri's eyes, I thought about how much I loved her. How much I desired her. How I wanted to drown in her.

So I did.

Azurine

PUP, MY SWEET, CHARMING boy, struggled on the ground. Tremors wracking his body. Eyes wide and filled with fear. One look—that was all we shared before I watched the light fade around him. His aura dimming. His life-force ebbing.

He collapsed. Head hitting the ground, body still.

My knees met grass and dirt.

"No." The word left me on a whisper—soft, dissipating as the waves of sound met the air around us. Slowly at first, terrified to be right, I crawled toward Pup. My eyes refusing to leave his body.

Not when Scarlett's quiet words brushed against my ears.

"By the Goddess, Amber. What did you do?"

Not when Rebel yelled out his confusion.

"What the fuck happened? Spook never touched him."

Not even when Beast's roar of anguish made the ground shake beneath my knees.

"No." I kept my eyes pinned to his chest. Praying. Chanting. Begging.

Just a breath. A single movement of air. That was all I needed to see. All I wished for.

A crack formed inside of me. A deep, dark chasm of pain and loss.

Louder, more angry. Malevolent. Violent in its destruction.

"No."

Clawing and pulling; ripping my soul apart as it separated me from Pup.

"No!"

I scrambled to my feet. Running, sliding in the dirt as I finally reached his side. He was so still. I turned him over. Brought his head to my lap. With shaking hands, I wiped the dirt from his face. He shouldn't be covered in dirt.

"No, no, no."

But no matter how many times I chanted the word, no matter how much I didn't want to believe it, I knew. I knew deep down inside where only Pup had ever been. Knew like the waves knew the shore. Knew with a certainty that made me tremble.

Pup was gone.

The thread between us had broken in a most brutal fashion. The magick of my family ripping us apart. The force of our separating causing our bond to fray the full length of my half.

Leaving what was left of my soul tattered. Damaged.

Irreparable.

"What happened to him?" Rebel knelt beside me, holding his hands over Pup as if he didn't know what to do. And he probably didn't. I didn't. Magick had killed my soul mate, and I had no idea how to bring him back.

I didn't speak, didn't answer him. Didn't feel the need. I knew my sister had done this. I knew the loss of my Pup was due to my family and our magick. I knew I'd probably never find the strength to forgive her. And I'd be damned if I was going to be the one to tell anyone what happened.

"Zuri?"

"It's my fault."

"Fix it."

Voices danced around me, a cacophony of sound assaulting me, but I lent them no credence. Words no longer mattered. There were none to bring him back, none to pull him away from the afterlife. Words had no value to me. Nothing did.

"I thought he was attacking Rebel."

"Why did you use that spell?"

"Fix it."

Burning in the agony of being ripped in two, my soul curled inward. The pain spread. Fanning out from a center point, rolling over everything in its way. Nothing to stop it. Nothing to soothe it. Nothing left. Nothing.

"What the hell is that?"

"It's Zuri. Her grief is causing a storm to build."

Black. Tied around his wrist. The headband I'd knotted. A spell I'd trusted. But it hadn't been enough. Childish string magick couldn't ward off an attack the likes of which Amber had dealt.

Huge tears fell from my face, wetting Pup's chest as I

bent over him. Trying to hold them back. My efforts in vain. Dropping my forehead to his chest, I sobbed. Great, gasping breaths rocked me. My cries matched by the scream of the wind through the trees. My tears met with a deluge of rain. Mother Nature mourned with me, wailing her pain as I did mine. Exploding in the agony we shared. I welcomed her. Welcomed her energy around me. Welcomed her anger and her violence, her pain and her loss. For hers couldn't even begin to compare with mine.

"Why is she doing this?"

"He's her red thread, Amber. You destroyed half of her soul right in front of her. What would you expect her to do?"

"By the Gods, she's going to flood the whole town."

Stabbing, violent pain washed over me, dragging me under a wave of darkness and grief. There was nothing left. Nothing. My family had served me the ultimate betrayal. My Pup was gone to the Summerlands without me. And my magick couldn't bring him back. I had nothing. Nothing but the wind and the rain and the waves. Drowning me in pain. Pulling what was left of my soul in an undertow of grief.

"Fix it."

"I didn't know."

"Fix it!"

Silence. Beast's pain-filled roar making even Mother Nature pause in her destructive mourning. Breaking through to me, making me take notice of those around me. One breath, two. Then Amber's hoarse whisper.

"I don't know how."

Suddenly, there was someone by my side. Warm and familiar, she grabbed my hand and whispered words that made sense to some part of my brain. Words of healing and renewal. The prayer of a faith so very different from mine.

"He's gone." I choked, wailing to the winds again. They

wailed back just as loud, the tears of their grief mixing with mine.

"I know." Charlotte put her arm around my shoulder, offering the comfort of her touch.

Beast sank to his knees across from me, eyes so vibrant they nearly glowed. "Bring him back."

I met his gaze, both of us tortured with grief, neither ready to let go.

"I can't."

My heart nearly stopped as I admitted my failing. I was no necromancer, no woman able to raise the dead from their graves or communicate with spirits. No witch with the power to control multiple elements at once. I was just Zuri, Azurine Weaver, water witch. I held no dominion over death.

"You have to." Beast looked down at Pup, an aching sadness sliding over his face. "He's my boy, my family. You need to bring him back."

"I don't know how."

We stared, mirroring our suffering to the other. I'd lost my love, my heart, my soul—Beast had lost the boy he saw as his family, his brother, his son. Two very different types of pain, both completely and utterly overwhelming.

"Beast, what are you…" Rebel paused, watching as Beast pulled Pup's head from my lap.

"I'm not giving up on him now." Beast turned Pup's still form, exposing the back of his neck. "I fixed him once."

"That was a changing bite. I don't think—"

Amber sank down beside me, reaching out to touch Pup's shoulder. "Let me try to fix it, Zuri. I know I fucked up; I didn't know he was your thread. Please let me try."

"Three witches and a werewolf." Scarlett joined us in the dirt and mud, sitting beside Pup's knees. "If this wasn't so dire, it'd make one hell of a good joke."

"If this works, I'm totally going to expect you to tell me it later, Zippo." Beast dropped his head back and spread his arms wide, looking to the sky as he released a growl. One I'd never heard before. Louder, fuller, and deeper, this growl warned the world about the strength of the person performing it.

His body shook as fur began to sprout. Black covering the painted skin, tattoos disappearing. His mouth lengthening almost to a snout. His ears moving up the sides of his head. Grotesque yet beautiful, unbelievable yet close enough to touch. He stopped shifting when he was at what appeared to be the halfway point. Half human, half wolf. Reeking of power and something that felt very much like magick.

"We have to work together." Scarlett scooted closer, barely able to keep her eyes off the wolf-man in our midst. "Amber, you start."

I sat back on my heels, fingers wrapped tightly around the black failure circling his wrist, the pull of my grief too heavy to fight. Meanwhile, my sisters worked in concert. Scarlett's fire magick warmed me and blanketed Pup. I could hear the wind turn as Amber directed it. Even the pull of my water magick—the swirling, pulsing waves of it—made itself known. My fingers itched to do…something. Cast, call, spell. But it was no use. My soul was torn, damaged beyond repair with the death of my thread. Not even magick could fix that. I sank into my grief, crying as my body shook.

But then a slap knocked me to the side.

"Bitch, help us." Scarlett stared at me, her eyes bright. And soaking wet. All around me, rain fell in a downpour that drowned the land and made it impossible to see more than a few feet. But where Pup and I rested—in the center of this chaos—was a perfect little circle of dryness. The eye of my storm.

"What can we do?" I swallowed as I looked down on Pup's body. I wanted to touch him, to run my fingers over his skin and feel the way his muscles twitched. But I knew he'd be still if I reached for him. Cold. Gone.

I curled my hands in my lap.

"I'm going to have to bite him, Zuri." Beast held Pup still, his hands on either side of his head to expose the back of his neck. "It's how I turned him from human to wolf shifter. He was almost dead; I didn't know…" His voice trailed off, his eyes going to Pup's still form. "It worked last time."

The wind picked up, Amber chanting under her breath and spreading her fingers over Pup's back. Over his lungs.

"Amber?" Scarlett said, looking to our sister.

"I'm trying, I swear I'm trying, but the air won't go."

As my sisters chanted, focusing their magick on my fallen soul mate; as Beast growled and bent over Pup's neck; as Rebel and Charlotte gripped my shoulders, offering me the only support they could; I surrendered. Gave up. Let go.

Leaning over Pup, my forehead brushing Beast's shoulder, I kissed the cheek of my dead lover.

"Wait in the Summerlands for me." A breath in, a tear, a final goodbye. "I love you, Adam. I always will."

SEVENTEEN

DARKNESS. SILENCE. I FLOATED in a void. A world of nothing. No sensory input, no feeling, no anything.

I'd always thought death would be an ending. Not some pop culture version of Heaven or Hell, no angels singing or pearly gates, no devils and flames. I assumed, when death came for me, it'd be lights-out. No more Adam. No more consciousness.

But I was aware. Awake.

And scared.

"No."

Zuri's voice tickled my ears, a whisper in the roar of the silence surrounding me. She sounded so lost, so broken. I wanted to find her, to seek her out and comfort her. But there was too much nothing to move. To fight. I floated on.

"No."

Maybe this was my own version of Hell. Again and again, she repeated her denial, her voice growing louder and more pained. The blackness smothered my sounds, ate my words. I was lost, listening to her grief with no way to help her. To comfort her. Her voice ripped my heart apart, shredding it with every no. Killing me syllable by syllable.

"He's gone."

Light. Blinding in its intensity. My feet on solid ground, a wind blowing across my skin. I shaded my eyes with my hand and looked around the world that had appeared out of nothing.

Grassy hills rolled on as far as I could see, meeting a perfect cornflower blue sky at the horizon. Winds swept across the sea of green, bending the blades, creating waves of dark and light. No buildings marred the landscape; no roads cut through the verdant fields; no signs of people on the oddly vibrant land.

Until I turned.

"I can't"

She stood only a few feet away, her long, dark hair blowing in the breeze. Beautiful, she could have been an older version of my mate. They shared the same almond-shaped jade eyes, the deep golden complexion that spoke of a Latin heritage. Her pink lips tipped up in a smile, one so familiar, it made my heart ache to see it. To see the single dimple appear in her cheek.

"Welcome to the Summerlands, Pup of the Feral Breed. I am Ximena Weaver." Her voice was soft and kind, something about it making me feel at peace. At least for a moment.

"Where's Zuri?"

Ximena cocked her head, appraising me, black hair falling over her shoulder in shiny waves. "She's back in the realm of your existence, of course. Her heart still beats. But yours does not."

"I want to go back." My voice came out slightly hoarse, my words choked.

"Yes, I imagine so. It wasn't quite your time, was it, young one? My daughters made a few mistakes."

She looked over my shoulder, making me turn. Across the field, three small girls played in the grass. Each one beautiful, looking so much like the woman before me that there was no doubt as to who they were.

"I don't know how."

Ximena smiled at the children as they laughed. "My girls were blessed with the power of the elements before they ever took their first breaths, but that power comes with responsibilities."

I watched as the young girl who looked like my Zuri raced in a circle, grabbing the hand of the smallest girl. Zuri and Scarlett, together even in this odd place.

"What responsibility does magick require?"

"Equality." Ximena watched as two girls played and the third looked our way. "Magick must have balance. It must be equal on all sides. Azurine and Scarlett are balanced against each other. Fire and water, opposite powers that keep the other in check. But my Amber…"

The third girl roamed closer, skipping through the grass in a zigzag pattern. Ximena grinned as the girl came closer, her face a perfect picture of motherly love.

"Amber is a powerful air witch, but she is unbalanced. I left the girls with Sarah Bishop so my oldest daughter would have a chance to grow up with an earth witch, to balance against the power of the mother. But Sarah's time is up. Already, we wait for her arrival. And when she goes, Amber will be alone. Unbalanced. Dangerous."

The little girl who must have been child Amber walked right up to me, eyes wide and pink lips turning up in a smile. Another Weaver woman with an adorable dimple hidden behind small smiles and tan cheeks.

"She knows you." Ximena's voice was soft, a quiet declaration filled with hope. "Amber feels your innate earth power."

I frowned as Amber reached for my hand, her little fingers gripping my larger ones. "I'm not a witch."

"What do we do?"

"No, but you carry the wolf within. Spirit of the earth and consort to earth witches. You have the ability to ground Amber.

Keep her safe. Keep her balanced."

Amber grinned, showing me a bright smile that made my heart begin to melt.

"But Zuri's my mate," I whispered. Confusion made me quiet, kept my voice hostage.

Ximena must have understood why I was hesitant.

"Weavers are never singular entities, Adam. We are linked—tied together through the thread of life. Just as you and Azurine are tied together."

Ximena stepped closer, bringing her hand up as if to touch the young Amber, but pulling away at the last moment. "You have a thread around you, one leading to Azurine. But Azurine has three such threads. The one to you, and two to her sisters. All linked together. To have one, you must take them all. They need each other. Are bound to each other. They are one."

Terrified of her answer, I confessed my truth. "But only Zuri's my mate; she's the only woman I want or will ever love. Her sisters..."

"I'm not talking about mates and love." Ximena laughed, obviously entertained by my assumption. "I'm talking about friendship. Partnership. Family. My girls all need you in their life, young one: Zuri as her lover and soul mate, Scarlett as her friend, and Amber as the person to keep her balanced and connected to the world. Without you, each will fall. Starting with Amber."

She crouched down before Amber, their eyes meeting, bright smiles lighting up both of their faces. "Already, a thread grows between you and Amber. One of family. One to tie you and her closer. To balance the magick between you."

She stood, a deep longing on her face even as she continued to smile at the young Amber. "Without you, each girl will die."

"No." My dead heart leapt, beating a violent rhythm in my chest. "I don't want Zuri to die. I don't want any of them to die."

Ximena stood, a smile on her lips. "Then make your pledge, young one. Tie yourself to all three. A lover to Azurine; a friend to Scarlett; and a brother to Amber."

I swallowed, nerves making my stomach clench. Too afraid to hope. "And then I can go back?"

Ximena nodded. "If that is your wish."

I looked her in the eye and made my pledge loud and clear.

"Yes. I want to go back. I want to be with Zuri."

Ximena's eyes grew bright with excitement as the world around me began to fade. "Do you swear to keep my girls together? To be the final element that will bring them balance?"

The girls disappeared, the light fading in the sky. "Yes. Yes, I swear it. I'll be their balance. I'll find a way."

The landscape disappeared, throwing me back into the vast emptiness I'd floated in before coming to meet Zuri's mother. But this time there was feeling, the sensation of air rolling over my skin. Of water rushing past my body. Of heat and warmth.

"Wait in the Summerlands for me."

"Zuri!" I struggled against the darkness but to no avail. As I rolled and fought against the nothing around me, Ximena's voice cut through the sound of the wind whipping past.

"Thank you, Adam Tackett of the Feral Breed. Thank you for your promise. You may go back to the realm you came from. The Summerlands will wait for you." A pause, a moment of quiet, and then a final whisper.

"Take care of my babies."

The winds increased, the feeling of flying through air growing stronger. My heart raced at a speed that surely would have broken me as a human. I closed my eyes, preparing for something, anxiously waiting for—

"I love you, Adam. I always will."

I WOKE WITH A gasp, desperate and terrified. My body moved without thought, reaching out in the direction of the tug on my heart, searching for proof that she was there. And when my fingers hit flesh, I dared for a single moment to hope. To dream of the only thing I wanted. To pray for soft golden skin to meet mine.

And it did.

Growling, I sat up and pulled Zuri into my lap. Clinging to her, shaking in relief as I breathed in her unique scent. She wrapped me in her arms, crying and squeezing me to the point of pain. But I didn't care. I was back; I was back and she was safely in my arms.

"Pup." She tilted her head back as she gasped my name, and the sight of her tear-stained face wrecked me. I pulled her closer, wrapping myself around her. Needing her body against mine.

"Jesus, Zuri. I thought I'd never make it back to you."

She sobbed harder as she clung to my shoulders.

"You died. I thought I'd lost you forever."

I pulled her tighter, needing to feel her as much as she needed to feel me. "Not even death can keep me away from you."

"By the gods…" Rebel's voice captured my attention. I glanced up to find him and Beast looking shocked and more than a little scared. Charlotte hung off Rebel's side, her eyes red and her cheeks streaked with the tracks of her tears. And, oddly enough, they were all soaking wet.

"You guys go swimming or something?"

A strained chuckle sounded before Rebel coughed. "No, your mate made it storm."

I glanced at the ground, noting how I felt dry, as did Zuri. "You sure about that?"

"It's a grief thing." Scarlett sat back, her face pale, her body language speaking of exhaustion. "Damn, Zuri, I didn't realize you could pull such a strong storm."

"Neither did I," Zuri mumbled against my chest. I pulled her closer, wrapping as much of my body around her as I could.

She trembled in my arms. "You're back."

I kissed the top of her head as the truth of her words washed over me.

"I am."

"How did you come back?"

Shrugging, I answered as honestly as I could. "I made a promise."

She pulled away, leaning back to meet my gaze. "What kind of promise?"

I leaned in to press my lips to hers, softly, reverently. "One to take care of you, to protect you, and to drag your sisters along with us, whether they like it or not."

Her smile was confused, beautiful, and way too kissable to resist. I took her bottom lip between my teeth and tugged, drawing out a moan from my girl.

"I heard you, you know." I slid my tongue into her mouth, tasting her, desperation growing inside of me. "I heard you say you loved me."

She pulled away and met my eyes, peering at me in a most serious way. "I meant it, you know."

I nodded. "I do know. And I mean them, too. I love you, Azurine Weaver. I always will."

I kissed her, long and deep, aggressively seeking a reconnection to my mate. She responded, matching me stroke for stroke. The laughter that went up around us and the yips of my teammates did nothing to stop me. I was back, and my mate was safe. Nothing else mattered.

EIGHTEEN

"WELL, THIS HAS BEEN a real hoot," Scarlett stood from her place on the forest floor, brushing the dirt from her pants. "I'm heading back to the lighthouse for the night. I need a bottle of tequila and a quiet room to process what the hell just happened here."

"Me too." Amber stood on shaky legs, avoiding eye contact with everyone. "I'm exhausted."

"I'll walk you over," Beast said. "I know Spook's dead, but I don't feel comfortable with you two traipsing through the woods alone."

"I'd be down for that plan but for one problem." Scarlett stretched and smirked at the shifter.

"What's that, Zippo?" Beast crossed his arms over his chest and raised his eyebrows in question.

"You have no clothes, old man."

Scarlett pointed at Beast's naked hip area and grinned. Beast just shrugged, not at all uncomfortable with his nudity.

"Either you get this studly, naked body to walk with, or I can shift to wolf. You decide."

"Wolf, please," Scarlett laughed, as Amber shook her head.

"I've seen enough of your junk for one day."

"Zuri?"

Amber took a step in my direction. She stopped long before she could reach me, her face filled with regret. "I'm really sorry. To you too, Pup. I never meant for that to happen."

She crossed her arms and curled in on herself, looking as if she wanted to cry. Before I could do more than frown at the confusion I felt in regards to her, Pup looked her way.

"You made a mistake, but it's not one that's unforgivable." He turned back to me, a small smile spreading across his handsome face. "We're all tied together. We have to be able to make mistakes, apologize for them, and be forgiven. That's what family does."

I smiled back, not ready to forgive her but understanding his words. We *were* tied together. By bonds of mating or sisterhood, threads or blood, the four of us were a unit. One I wasn't willing to break from.

I broke my gaze with Pup to turn toward my sister. "We'll come to see Sarah in the morning. I'd like to make tonight about Pup, if that's okay."

There was no sound for a moment, but then Amber nodded, her voice sincere as she said, "Okay. And maybe you could help me contact the coven tomorrow...let them know it's safe to come back."

"Sure. I'd be happy to help."

Pup grinned at me, making my own lips tug up into what felt like a huge smile.

"C'mon, kids," Beast said as he put an arm around each of my sisters. "Let's leave these two alone. That adrenaline is going to wear off soon, and they're going to get a little freaky. A wolf reconnecting with his mate is not something you want to witness. Unless you're into that kind of thing."

"I thought you were going to go all fuzzy?" Scarlett laughed as Amber yanked out of his hold.

"Eh, I like the brisk, November wind on my balls. Makes me feel alive. And hey, boss?" Beast gave Rebel a serious look. "I'll take care of the burning tonight. Just leave old Spook where he lies for now."

Beast ran off into the woods, singing loudly in a language I didn't recognize. Amber and Scarlett followed him down the trail, whispering to each other as they went.

"We're going to stick with you two." Rebel walked over, poor Charlotte still tucked under his arm. "We'll hang at the campsite for the night, just in case. I can't"—he looked away, breathing harder for a few moments—"I can't risk any more right now. I need to know you're both okay."

His statement, while seemingly innocent, carried a weight to the words that made my stomach drop. Pup had died; I'd mourned him to the point of unconsciously pulling a storm over the region; and we'd pronounced our love for one another.

I didn't know if okay was a word I'd use to describe anything about us.

"I've got my mate." Pup shrugged and smiled at me, calming my anxiety in an instant. "The threat's gone, I beat death, and she loves me. How much more okay could I be?"

"All right. We'll be at the cottage all night. But call Charlotte if you need us. I dropped my phone in the sink and haven't made it to the store for a new one yet."

Pup's smile fell, looking irritated all of a sudden. "Now you tell me."

Rebel cocked his head in question, but Pup ignored him. Pulling me to my feet instead. "C'mon, mate. Let's go home."

WALKING UP THE STEPS to our little cabin was surreal. It seemed as if weeks had passed since I'd been on the wooden porch, yet it had been less than two hours. Two hours in which we came face-to-face with a deranged man obsessed with my sister, Pup died, and three witches and a shifter brought him back to life.

Okay, so surreal didn't even begin to cover it.

I walked inside first, looking around at the small space. It was homey here, warm and welcoming. As soon as Pup shut the door, I slid my leggings down my legs. I wanted to be comfortable, to curl up with Pup and just…be. Sans pants.

Kicking the fabric to my bag, I took a step toward the bathroom but was caught up in Pup's arms. Spinning and directing me to the corner, he pushed me against the wall, caging me in with his arms. Shaking as he pressed his body along the length of mine.

Even without words, I knew what this was. Fear. As much as I'd almost lost Pup, he'd almost lost me as well. And that level of pain and fear was not something easily brushed away.

I leaned into Pup's hold, gripping his shoulders. "Are you okay?"

"No." He pulled me tighter, breathing into my hair. "I panicked when I couldn't reach you. I thought…I thought… hell, I don't want to think of what I thought."

I ran my hands up and down his back. "I know. When you died—"

I choked on the word, still unable to think about that moment without being swamped by grief.

"Baby." Pup lifted my chin and captured my gaze with his. "Calm down. You're going to make it rain inside."

"Sorry." I closed my eyes for a moment, reveling in his touch and soaking up his heat.

"I'm here, baby," he whispered. "We're here."

We stood that way for several minutes, clinging to one another as our fear and separation anxiety settled. The longer I held him, the more brazen I became. The more aroused. Having him so big and warm and right there against me was something I couldn't resist. My hands wandered of their own accord… down his arms, around his waist, over his hips to cup his ass.

He groaned my name and pushed himself against me. His big hands wrapped around my waist, kneading, fingers slipping and pulling at the hem of the shirt I wore.

"You're in my sweatshirt." It wasn't a question, but a statement. Simple and clean.

"I missed you. I wanted your scent on me."

He brought his lips to my neck, kissing and licking his way to my shoulder. "I gave you a claiming mark; my scent is all over you. It's inside of you. Every inch of you smells like me."

He stopped and pulled away, that same nervous and guilty look from earlier in the day on his face. "It's why they kicked you out, Zuri. Your coven could smell me on you, the wolf in me. It's my fault they banished you."

"Oh." It was all I could say, all I had within me. Pup had bitten me that first morning, which had kicked off the banishment. But after fighting with Amber and hearing the hurt I'd caused her, I knew he was wrong. Nothing about what my coven had done was his fault; it was mine.

"I'm so sorry, Zuri."

"Don't. Don't you apologize. You did nothing wrong."

"I should have told you about the bite, what it means. I'm bound to you forever. I can sense you, find you. You're in my blood now."

I pulled his face to mine. Licked his lip. Kissed his jaw. "And how do I return the favor?"

My question stopped him. He stood, unmoving. I watched his eyes, looking for some sign of what I'd said that was wrong.

"Pup?"

He licked his lips, his eyes still dark with his arousal and the hard length of him pressing against my stomach.

"You want to be my mate? Forever?"

I grinned. "You're my red thread, the other half to my soul. If there's some kind of ritual we need to do so you feel the same connection to me that I feel to you, I'm in."

"I thought you'd be mad," he murmured.

"I'm mad that you didn't tell me, that you made me worry with your guilt and your silence. But I'm not mad that you bonded us." I leaned forward, licking up the length of his neck. "I've been nothing but in need of you since the first time I saw you. So tell me what I have to do."

"To complete the mating, to make it permanent"—he licked his lips again as his body gave a sudden shudder—"you'd have to bite me."

I traced the length of his neck where the shadow of a few of the hickeys I'd left him remained. Not as dark as mine still were.

"But I have bitten you."

He shook his head. "You'd have to draw blood."

I nodded once, thoughts of his blood mingling with mine oddly more enticing than I would have imagined. As a witch, I was well aware of blood magick and the mixed connotations about it. I knew the Parity Lake coven was staunchly against blood magick, fearing it opened a door to the darker side of magick. But this was about bonding myself to my soul mate, the one the Fates selected for me. That couldn't be dark.

"You don't have to if you don't want to."

Pup's soft voice pulled me from my own thoughts. His face was drawn, his eyes cast down. Disappointed.

"It's not that I don't want to bond myself to you, but blood magick—"

"It's not magick."

I smiled. "Everything is magick. From the wind in the

trees to the way the ground beneath our feet feeds the crops. Everything about this world is infused with magick. You are magick." I ran my hands over his chest and down his flat stomach. "The bond between us is magick." I pressed lower, hands sliding over him as I worked my way around to his hips and thighs. "When we're together, we create magick."

He groaned and pulled me into his arms, fastening his mouth over mine. The kiss was clumsy at first, too heated and needy, but we quickly smoothed it out. Lips and tongues moved together, dancing and sliding as our breaths turned to pants. Pup's hand went right to the edge of his sweatshirt, pushing the fabric up as he worked his way up my thighs. When he reached my panties, he didn't pause. He pushed them down off my hips and down my legs. I stepped out of them, never breaking our kiss, my hands too busy holding him to me to worry about where the garment ended up.

Pup grabbed my ass, squeezing, letting his fingers tickle my pussy from behind. I moaned into his mouth and gasped as he slid one finger inside of me, just deep enough to want more.

"You're so damn wet."

I nodded, biting his shoulder as he slid a second finger inside. He pushed and stretched, playful and teasing.

"Pup, please."

"I like this look, by the way." His voice was warm and thick like syrup, coating me in his sweetness. "The knee socks and sweatshirt are very eighties-cool. Plus I like seeing you in my clothes."

"You do?" I gasped again as his thumb pressed against a place no one had been, exerting pressure and making my legs shake.

"Of course." He licked his way over my jaw, down to my neck, where he sucked hard enough for me to curse in response. "You wearing my clothes may be the hottest damn thing I've ever seen in my life."

"Oh." My entire body shook as he worked his fingers deeper inside me, that errant thumb still pressing *there*. I clung to his arms, desperate for more but afraid to voice what I wanted. In case he stopped. I never wanted him to stop.

"You have my permission to wear anything you want of mine, anytime." He ran his teeth along my collarbone.

"I'll wear your clothes every day if it makes you—"

My breath hitched as he slid a third finger inside of me, the delightful burn of the stretch stealing my thoughts.

"If it makes me what?"

"Fuck." Legs shaking, I clung to him. "If it makes you want me this much."

"I always want you. Every second. I do nothing but want you." He leaned down and brushed the sweetest, softest kiss against my lips before whispering, "I'm positively starving for you."

"Then have me."

Without warning, he picked me up and carried me across the room. He laid me on the bed, the delicateness of his hands and movements an example of how caring he was. Legs hanging over the edge of the mattress, I started to scooch forward, but he placed one arm across my waist and held me down. With his other hand, he reached underneath me and lifted my hips off the mattress.

Sliding my fingers under the soft fabric covering me, I pulled his sweatshirt up over my hips and stomach. He licked his lips as my legs fell open, revealing myself to him. A single pause, a moment of perfect, teasing tension as he stared at all I revealed to him, and then his mouth was on me. Hot and wet and perfect, he sucked my clit and flattened his tongue against me. My head fell back, hands clutching the blanket, whispered cries and moans falling from my lips. This wasn't gentle. No, this was not a delicate man taking his time and cherishing the feel of his woman on his lips. This was a man dying of thirst and finally finding an oasis in a world of sand. A man desperate and needy. He'd said he was starving for me; the way he tried to devour me proved it.

Over and over he sucked and lapped, groaning as he moved from clit to labia and back. Nibbling, licking, diving inside. And all the while, I angled my hips and gripped his hair and refused to let him break away. Not that he tried to. But I wanted more. I always wanted more of my Pup. I wanted the release I knew he'd give me. I wanted the feel of his teeth in my flesh. I wanted his tongue inside me when I came. I wanted to see him drenched in me.

His arm across my waist kept me from sliding away as he spread my legs wider and continued to feast on me. Pressure inside me grew; as the orgasm I'd been chasing came into view, I thrashed on the bed. But when that buildup finally peaked and the deep, throbbing need threatened to split me open, he released my hips and let me move as I wanted. As I needed. I pulled his face into my pussy and rode his mouth as my body contracted, loving the way he slid his tongue inside me. Licking, sucking, groaning; the vibrations only adding to the sensation.

"Good goddamn, baby." Pup lifted me, stripping me of his shirt even as he pushed me up the mattress. I didn't stop him, my body too blissed out and jellylike to do much more than hum. Within seconds, he hovered over me, naked. I wrapped my legs around his hips to bring him closer, loving the way his dick slid against my swollen flesh.

But as he started to slide inside, I pushed on his chest. "Wait."

He froze, breathing hard but not moving. "Why? What's wrong?"

I shook my head and smiled as I pushed on his one shoulder.

He rolled slowly, cautiously, as if afraid I was going to push him away and make a run for it. Instead, I straddled his thighs as soon as he was on his back and rolled my hips along the length of his dick.

"I want to be on top."

His smile was slow and easy, filled with a casual masculinity that drove me crazy.

"By all means, baby. Ride me."

I started slow, sliding along his length, teasing him. But after only a few passes, I grew tired of waiting. With an angle of my hips and a slow glide back, I pushed onto him. The stretch and the fullness had me lifting myself to sitting and letting my head fall back. So good, so thick. I rocked experimentally, loving the way the head of his dick pressed against something delicious and exciting inside of me. I moved in a rhythm all my own, rocking into the pleasure, spreading my lips with my fingers and teasing my clit as I leaned farther back.

"Jesus, Zuri." Pup's groan brought me back to the present, to the knowledge that the man under me was enjoying this just as much as I was. I pulled up with a smile, loving the way he dragged his fingers down my lips to spread me farther as his dick nearly slid out of me. Then I sat back hard, driving him up, taking him deep. He bit his lip and groaned as his head fell back. So I did it again. And again.

Soon, we were a rocking, plunging, cursing, sweating mass of sensation. I could hardly pay attention to him. My own pleasure so strong and powerful, I barely noticed his. He thrust his hips in time with mine, never releasing me, keeping his thumbs on either side of my clit to give me even more sensation.

"Shit, gonna come." He pushed hard, pulled me tighter as I swiveled my hips and grabbed one of his hands. I entwined our fingers and brought our joined hand between my legs, pressing our knuckles against my clit to get the pressure I so desperately needed.

"Fuck, Zuri. Fuck. Yes."

With a shiver and a groan, I reached that peak of release. My entire body pulsed as Pup thrust a few more times, reaching his own climax with a loud snarl. Our bodies covered in sweat. Our breaths coming in pants.

He stayed inside me as I came down, my breathing leveling out. After a few minutes of snuggling and casual affection, he smiled up at me. Feeling a wetness cooling against my thighs, I sighed.

"We made a mess."

Pup glanced down between us. "Don't care."

"No?"

"Not a bit."

I leaned over and licked his lips. "You get me so wet."

"And I love it."

And with that, he rolled me underneath him. He deepened the kiss, his tongue exploring my mouth in a way that was pure sin. When we broke, he pulled back with a grin more vibrant than any I'd seen before.

"My name's Adam Tackett, and you, Azurine Weaver, are the love of my life."

I smiled, a happiness I'd never experienced flowing through my heart. "You remembered."

He nodded. "Someone very important helped me. She mentioned my name. I was so focused on getting back to you that I didn't even notice it at the time, but now..."

He trailed off, still grinning, still watching me, his eyes filled with emotion.

"We're tied," he said, voice quiet but confident. "You and me, your sisters. The four of us are a unit now. One I intend to honor and respect. And maybe one day, when we've known each other for more than a couple of days"—he grinned, and I grinned back—"maybe you'll tie yourself to me with more than metaphorical thread. Maybe we'll use rings and promises and the sharing of a name. My name."

He touched his lips to mine, all warm and soft. And as I lay in his arms, in that tiny bed, in a crappy little cabin with plywood walls, I knew I was exactly where I belonged.

Home.

NINETEEN

I DROPPED THE LAST of the boxes from the lighthouse on the porch, grinning as I saw Zuri inside putting her things away.

"I think that's everything."

Rebel leaned against the front of his truck, giving me a sarcastic smile. "I sure as hell hope so. Two truckloads of shit—good luck fitting all that into your little apartment when you come back to the city."

I shrugged. "We'll work it out."

"You sure you're going to be okay with this?" Rebel had that appraising look on his face, inspecting me as was his usual. "I don't want to leave you out here alone if you think you may need our help."

"It's just temporary." I leaned against the porch railing. "We'll stay here to spend as much time as we can with Sarah while we can. The girls need that. And then, when Sarah moves on to the Summerlands, we'll head to Detroit and figure out what to do from there."

Rebel shook his head. "A mate and her two sisters. I don't know, man. You've got more guts than I do."

I glanced to where my girl was standing, both sisters at her side, the three of them laughing with Charlotte over something. "Zuri's a package deal. She's worth any headache the other two bring my way. Besides"—I looked him in the eye, making sure he understood the seriousness behind my words—"I made a promise to someone. I owe them."

Rebel stared at me for a long moment, the eye contact not making either of us uncomfortable. I hadn't told anyone about my visit to the Summerlands, not even Zuri. It wasn't really an intentional decision to keep it a secret. But when I tried to explain what had happened while I'd been dead, the words wouldn't come. Maybe I wasn't supposed to say. Or maybe it was a moment just for me and Ximena. Something personal and private between a mother and the man who would spend the rest of his life protecting her daughters.

Whatever it was, I hadn't said, and no one had pushed me on it. Not even my mate.

"So, you're staying here?" Charlotte asked as Zuri and her sisters joined us. I gave Amber a noogie because I knew how much it pissed her off. Ximena said to be a brother to her; seemed to me being an annoying one was like respecting my pledge and having fun at the same time.

Amber shoved me, throwing her head back. "You're such an ass."

"Yeah, but your sister digs that ass. She thinks it's hot."

"I do." Zuri came up beside me. I wrapped my arms around my mate and buried my face in her neck, still so relieved to have her safely in my arms again. "Though it's not my favorite part of him."

Zuri and Charlotte giggled as Rebel groaned. "Too much information, Zuri."

"No such thing as TMI," Scarlett said. "So we know these two are going to be fucking like bunnies in the cabin"—she thrust her thumb in our direction—"but where are you two off to, Charlotte?"

"We're headed to Detroit for a few days, and then I'll be going back to Milwaukee." Charlotte glanced over her shoulder at Rebel, both looking almost giddy but nervous at the same time. "Julian still has a few months of school left, so we'll be doing the long-distance thing until his semester ends. But then we're talking about moving in together. In Detroit."

Everyone cheered. Even knowing how hard it would be on Rebel to be separated from his mate, the fact that Charlotte and Julian would eventually be moving in with him was good. Rebel didn't need any more uncertainty in his relationship with Charlotte. As the group began to settle down, Beast strolled up and threw an arm over Scarlett's shoulders and looked at Rebel.

"What's so important in Detroit that you're dragging your mate over there just to send her back west?"

Rebel smiled. "I've got a few things to set up with the den, and they're things I have to do in person."

"Like what?" I asked.

"Like…a woman has asked to pledge the Breed, and I'm allowing it. Plus we'll have four mated members in the ranks."

I frowned. "Four? Me, you, Gates…who else?"

Rebel grinned. "Kaija."

My eyebrows rose as Rebel laughed.

"I know. But Gates called last night. He said she was ready and it's what she wants."

"A woman pledge." Beast shook his head and grinned. "I never thought I'd see the day. I can't believe Gates is going to let her ride."

"Let her?" Amber scowled at the hulking shifter. "Who is he to *let her*? Are you wolves complete Neanderthals? A woman can do what she wants, including riding around on a motorcycle."

"Here we go." Zuri chuckled against my chest. "He's going

to get her all riled up now."

I pushed my mate away from the group as they argued, sliding my hands into the back pockets of her jeans and squeezing her ass.

"How about, as soon as these guys leave, I get you all riled up?"

She leaned her head back and smiled up at me. "You going to take me for a ride, Pup?"

I growled, long and low as I brought my lips to hers. "You can ride me anytime, beautiful."

"Yo, Pup," Rebel yelled, making me jump. "I think you're missing something."

I glanced up to see Rebel and Beast standing on the far side of the vehicles, smiling.

"What's up?"

He waved, beckoning me. "Why don't you come here and find out?"

I glanced at Zuri, who simply shrugged. We walked over, holding hands, happy just to be together. It was an amazing feeling, knowing my mate loved me. Something warm and right, something I cherished. I pitied anyone who tried to take it away from me; even death itself wasn't strong enough to best me.

When I reached the guys, Rebel smiled and grabbed me by my shoulders.

"You've been a wonderful prospect, one of the best we've ever had. You've showed bravery and smarts, loyalty and heart. You've earned our respect as a man, as a shifter, and as a brother."

I swallowed hard, fighting a burn in my eyes as Rebel stepped back.

Beast smirked. "Yeah, yeah, you've earned our respect. But now it's time to earn that." He pointed across the field. A wooden stake had been planted in the ground, easily ten feet high. At the top, a vest hung. A black leather vest with a howling wolf insignia and two rockers on the back. The top rocker I'd had on my cut since I was made a prospect. It spelled out Feral Breed in a curve above the wolf. The other, sitting under the insignia, let everyone know my den home. Detroit.

"Fuck me."

"No time, Pup." Zuri grinned, obviously knowing what this was. "We're not going to make this easy on you, so you better run."

Flames erupted between me and the vest. A warm wind blew through the field, making the fire dance on the air. Storm clouds rolled in overhead, promising thunder and lightning as they darkened the morning sky.

"Damn, we should have gotten a couple of witches before." Beast smacked Rebel in the chest as they watched the girls put on a show. "This is way better than when we made Numbers wrestle that alligator."

"Hey Pup," Rebel yelled. "You've got three minutes to take it, man."

I immediately took off running, heading for the fire. While I didn't think Scarlett would purposely burn me, I knew earning that patch meant braving everything they threw at me. There were no shortcuts or cheats. If I was going to get it, I had to run straight through the challenges the girls threw at me.

Nearing the flames, now curving and arching high in the sky as Amber's wind fed them, I sped up. The heat burned my eyes and made it hard to catch my breath, but I kept running. Harder, faster, until finally diving past the wall of fire and rolling to a stop in front of the stake. Before I could reach for the vest, the sky above opened up. Thunder rumbled through the air, shaking the ground, and lightning struck a tree only a few yards away.

"My own mate is trying to kill me," I yelled, smiling as I

caught her eye from across the open field.

"Rebel said you had to work for it, baby." Zuri's grin was obvious in the tone of her voice. I rolled my eyes and shook my head as the rain began to fall, soaking me within seconds.

"I'm getting you back for this."

Zuri laughed. "I sure as hell hope so."

I examined the wood stake as the rain fell, wiping water from my face every few seconds. The vest was too high for me to reach, not even if I jumped. The rain made the stake too slick to climb, never mind the fact that it was too thin and weak-looking to hold me. There was only one way I could see to get my vest.

I took a step back, twisting my hips toward the stake.

"You'd better not let it fall, Pup," Rebel yelled. I waved a hand in the air, not needing the reminder. This vest was something to be cherished, honored. Letting it hit the ground was sacrilege to the Feral Breed.

I took a deep breath. I could do this. I was strong enough, fast enough, and nimble enough to do this. I just had to concentrate.

Releasing the breath I'd been holding, I shifted my weight, aimed, and kicked. As my foot made contact with wood, I threw my upper body forward, grabbing the stake right above the break and shoving it away from me. The top of the wood came down nearly on top of me, exactly as I planned, making the vest land safely in my hands.

Raucous cheers went up from across the field, and I grinned. My hands shook as I ran them over the vest, the leather smooth and new. As Rebel, Beast, and the girls ran over, I untucked the top and opened the fold. My fingers found the front panel, where a patch sat on the left side. Curved, with bold block letters spelling out my new name.

Phoenix.

"You've proven yourself long before today." Rebel walked up beside me, his arm wrapped around a smiling Charlotte. "You've earned that cut from the moment you pledged yourself, and I'm proud to be the one to put it on your back."

He came up behind me, taking the leather from my hands. I slipped my arms in as Rebel held it, so proud I had to blink back a burn in my eyes as he straightened the vest along my shoulders. Once finished, Rebel took a step back, joining the rest of my family forming an arc in front of me.

Beast stepped in front of the girls, beaming at me with what looked like pride. My friend and mentor, the man I'd looked up to for years, held a full leather jacket with the Breed insignia and rockers on the back as well as a skullcap matching his. All customized with my new name.

"My brother, my friend," Beast said. "You carry my spirit in you, my essence, and my brother's blood mixed with yours. You are family to me, pack, and you are one of a long line of brave protectors. I've never been prouder than I am today."

He handed me the folded jacket and cap, gripping my arm in a show of companionship and welcome. Rebel joined him, his long fingers wrapping around my bicep.

"Be proud, be brave, and be Feral. Welcome to the Feral Breed, Phoenix."

The girls clapped and cheered as I slipped into the jacket.

"Thank you." I shook hands with Rebel, unable to keep the smile off my face.

"I never doubted you, man."

I turned to Zuri, my mate, surrounded by her sisters and my brothers. My family—witches, shifters, and humans alike.

"I did it."

Zuri rushed to me, wearing the brightest smile I'd ever seen. "I knew you would, Phoenix."

Hearing her say my handle, my new Breed road name,

made my grin widen. Damn, it felt good to know I'd finally done it. I'd earned the respect of my denmates. And I'd finished that proving with my mate at my side.

"Enough sappiness," Rebel hollered with a smile. "It's time to head for the dirty D."

Beast, Amber, and Scarlett left for the lighthouse. He'd be staying with them and Sarah for the week, commuting to Yard Shark Customs. Even with Spook dead, none of us felt comfortable leaving the women alone. We could only guess why Spook had gone over the edge and fixated on Amber. We assumed it was because he'd been alone too long, having never found his mate. It happened more often than we'd like. But that didn't explain how he knew her, why he stalked her, or what inciting event pushed him to obsess over her.

The unanswered questions made all of us too nervous to leave them unprotected.

Rebel and Charlotte hopped into his truck and pulled out of the driveway, ready to begin their adventure in Detroit.

Leaving my mate and me alone.

Zuri grabbed me by the sides of my coat and tugged me down, placing a small kiss on the corner of my mouth. I grinned, still riding a high of finally achieving my goal. I had my club, my den, my brothers, my new family, and my mate. What more could I want?

Her kiss deepened for a moment, giving me the tiniest taste of her before she moved to whisper in my ear.

"You, me, the cabin, and no clothing except that hot as hell vest." She pulled back, smiling seductively and licking her lips. "I'm going to give you the dirtiest blow job known to man, wolf, or witch to celebrate."

Well…okay. I could want more of that.

THE FERAL BREED
SERIES INFORMATION

The Feral Breed Series consists of:

Claiming His Fate
Claiming His Need
Claiming His Witch

And look for new titles beginning in 2015:

Claiming His Beauty
Claiming His Fire
Claiming His Desire
Claiming Her Heart

Check out the Feral Breed Series Page on www.ellisleigh.com for the latest listing of novels, novellas, and short stories in the Feral Breed world.

ACKNOWLEDGMENTS

First and foremost, I want to say thank you to the readers of the Feral Breed. From the first book, you've made me so grateful to have the opportunity to share my stories with you. It's your excitement and appreciation that keeps me working so hard to write better and faster.

To Lisa, who answers my questions, cheerleads like only a Texas girl should know how to do, and keeps me from looking like I don't know the rules of grammar. Because I don't…not all of them. That's why you hire an editor like Lisa.

To Caren, who continues to be the bestest friend a girl could ask for. From calming my fears to turning around edits in record time, you make all of this so much easier.

To Esher, who makes me giggle-snort on a daily basis. Also, I'll never wear a gray shirt on a hot day again without wanting to yell "hot as balls."

To Heather, who dances in and out of my life but is never too far away.

To my husband, who continually reminds me to stop working and disconnect for awhile before I miss everything. And who makes me popcorn when I ask for it.

ACKNOWLEDGMENTS

To all the folks in the Feral Breed Reader Group, to my Twitter friends, and to the authors over at Romance Divas, thank you for keeping my world so broad. You deserve cookies for the entertainment, instruction, and motivation you've provided me.

Edited by Silently Correcting Your Grammar, LLC
Cover Art by Cormar Covers